75 SCA...

HORROR

STORIES

**Creepy, spooky and scary stories
that will give you nightmares!**

STEVEN PARKER

Steven Ronald Parker

Has asserted his right to be identified as the Author of this book.

All rights reserved.

Steven Ronald Parker owns the sole rights to his own literature submitted and published in this book.

This book is sold subject to the condition that it shall not by way of trade or otherwise be lent, resold, hired out, have any content removed and used, or be reproduced and/or transmitted by any means or otherwise circulated without the Author's prior consent, in any form or binding or cover than that in which it is published and without similar condition being imposed on the subsequent purchaser.

Ownership rights of Steven Ronald Parker, 2021

Published and Copyright © 2021

ISBN-13: 9798708375322

Other books by...

AUTHOR

Steven Parker

Religion

Why All Religions Are Wrong
ISBN: 9781490979564

Evil God
ISBN: 9798665438856

Humour

101 Ways To Avoid Work!
ISBN: 9781490515878

The Lazy Man's Guide To Women!
ISBN: 9781490534954

CONTENTS

Introduction   1

75 Scary Horror Stories

1.	The Caretaker	4
2.	The Wine Barrel	8
3.	The Hitchhiker	10
4.	Sticky Notes	17
5.	My Show	21
6.	The Accident	24
7.	The Tourist	26
8.	The Werewolf	32
9.	The Plan	35
10.	Seaweed	40
11.	The Phone Booth	42
12.	The Maid	46
13.	Wallpaper	49
14.	Natural Habitat	52
15.	The Best of Friends	56
16.	The Photographer	58
17.	The Light	60
18.	The Patient	63
19.	The Waiter	66
20.	Hide and Seek	68
21.	The Railway Crossing	71
22.	False Teeth	73

23.	The Politician's Daughter	77
24.	Handprints	81
25.	The Black Suit	84
26.	The Psychiatrist	86
27.	The Abandoned Mine	89
28.	The Keyhole	93
29.	Bad Brother	95
30.	The Time Traveller	97
31.	The Divorce	100
32.	The Photographs	104
33.	The Wheelchair	105
34.	The Decoy	108
35.	Paper Shapes	112
36.	The Strange Woman	114
37.	Reasonable Doubt	118
38.	The Earwig	125
39.	The Book of Evil	130
40.	The Bite	132
41.	The Attic	135
42.	The Wedding	138
43.	Bouquet of Flowers	141
44.	Piggyback	144
45.	The Endless Loop	148
46.	The Third Wish	150
47.	The Dilemma	152
48.	Wristbands	155
49.	Red Rope	157
50.	The Guesthouse	160

51.	Face to Face	163
52.	The Camera	165
53.	The Little Old Lady	168
54.	The Storage Room	171
55.	The Date	175
56.	The Psychic	178
57.	The Guard Dog	181
58.	The Vault	183
59.	The Clown	187
60.	The Unfrozen	189
61.	Top Brands	193
62.	The Button	196
63.	The Parents	200
64.	The Stairs	206
65.	The Intruder	208
66.	Shared Custody	211
67.	Little Red Pills	213
68.	Family Portraits	216
69.	Text Messages	218
70.	Hell	222
71.	Hit and Run	224
72.	The Clown Doll	227
73.	The Farm	230
74.	The Apartment	233
75.	Footprints	238

My Story	242

Are You Being Haunted?	244
Demons and Poltergeists	247
Traditional Ghosts	253
Goodnight	262
About the Author	265

INTRODUCTION

By choosing to read this book, you have now entered the world of the unnatural and the unknown - and you have chosen to pit your anxieties and your fears against the suspense, the chills and the horror of what awaits you inside.

Dare, if you will, to read slowly and carefully through each of the 75 scary horror stories contained within this book. These stories have been compiled via the Author's own vivid imagination and considerable research into the world of horror - so you can be assured that they will send a shiver down your spine and leave you reaching for all the light switches you can find!

Each story, in its own way, is scary, creepy and spooky - and they are all sure to leave you deeply disturbed and wondering exactly how YOU would cope in such a situation, were they true and actual real life events?

Imagine if these stories were true? Imagine if these stories were real? Can you even begin to put yourself in these situations? How would you cope emotionally? How would you react physically? If you found yourself in these situations, would you freeze? Would you keep your composure? Or would you run just as fast as you possibly can and never look back?

Aside from the 75 scary horror stories included within this book, there are also 90 very short horror stories that appear after each main story. These very short stories range from a single sentence to a short paragraph, but they show how horror can very easily arise with just a fleeting thought or a brief 'what if...' scenario.

While the 75 scary horror stories offer a twist and a 'sting in the tail', the 90 very short horror stories will offer the mind something quite terrifying to ponder.

Do not miss the spooky story from the Author's own personal experience on page 242 also. This story is based upon a real life event that, still to this very day, is a source of bewilderment for the Author.

As this book delves heavily into the world of the supernatural, the otherworldly and the presence of both malevolent and benevolent beings, the book concludes with a look at demons, poltergeists and other more friendly ghostly beings - and explains how you can know, and what you can expect, if you find that you or your home is being haunted by such entities.

Well let us not delay any longer! As promised, you have 75 scary horror stories ahead to test all of your nerves, and ultimately, your ability to switch off the bedside light and sleep peacefully. How will YOU fare?

Let us now find out...

75 SCARY HORROR STORIES

1

The Caretaker

A young woman called Megan was serving a life sentence in prison for murder. Feeling angry and resentful about her situation, she came to the conclusion that she simply could not spend the rest of her life behind bars, so she began plotting ways to escape.

Over time, she became good friends with the prison caretaker. One of his jobs was to bury the prisoners who had died in a graveyard just outside the prison walls. Whenever a prisoner died the caretaker would ring a 'death bell', that all the prisoners would hear, so they would know that one of their prison inmates had died. The caretaker then took the dead body and placed it in a coffin. Once the caretaker had filled out all the paperwork and the death certificate in his office, he would then return to the coffin and nail the coffin lid shut. Finally he would place the coffin on a wagon, take it to the graveyard and then bury it.

Knowing this routine, Megan carefully devised an escape plan and shared it with the caretaker. The caretaker agreed to slip her a copy of the key to her cell, and next time the bell rang, Megan would leave her cell and sneak into the dark room where the coffins are kept. She would then hide inside the coffin that contained the dead prisoner while the caretaker was filling out his paperwork and the death certificate. When the caretaker returned, he would nail the coffin lid shut and take it outside of the prison with Megan and the dead prisoner inside. He would then bury the coffin. The caretaker also agreed to slip her a lighter, so that she would not be in complete darkness the entire time.

Megan knew that there would be a sufficient amount of air in the coffin for her to breathe until later in the evening when the caretaker would return to the graveyard, under the cover of darkness, and dig up the coffin to set her free!

The caretaker was of course a little reluctant to go along with Megan's plan, but since both he and Megan had become such good friends over the years, he agreed to go along with her plan.

Megan waited several weeks for one of the other prison inmates to die. Then one night, while she was asleep in her cell, she finally heard the death bell ringing. So she got up, unlocked the door to her cell using the key that the caretaker had already given her, and walked down the hallway towards the room where the coffins were kept. She was nearly caught on a couple of occasions and her heart was beating fast, but she managed to make her way undetected.

She opened the door to the darkened room where the coffins were kept and, quietly and in the dark, she found the coffin that contained the dead body. She carefully climbed into the coffin, closed the coffin lid and waited for the caretaker to return to nail the lid shut.

It was not long before she heard footsteps coming, shortly followed by the pounding of nails being hammered into the coffin lid. Even though she was very uncomfortable sharing such a confined space with a dead body, she knew that with each nail being driven into the coffin, she was one step closer to freedom!

The coffin was then lifted onto the wagon and taken outside to the graveyard. She could feel the coffin being lowered slowly into the ground, and she was sure not to make a sound as the coffin hit the bottom of the grave with a gentle thud.

Finally she could hear the sound of dirt covering the wooden coffin, and she knew that it would only be a matter of time before she would be free at last! After several minutes of absolute silence, she began to chuckle quietly to herself.

Feeling curious, she decided to light the lighter that the caretaker had given to her and find out the identity of the dead prisoner she shared the coffin with. To her horror, she discovered that the dead body was that of the caretaker.

- A young girl is playing in her bedroom when she hears her mother call her name from the kitchen downstairs. As she is running down the hallway towards the top of the stairs, she is dragged into her mother's bedroom. It's her mother, who whispers to her "don't go downstairs honey, I heard that too!"

2

The Wine Barrel

There was a married couple called Lewis and Abigail who both came from exceedingly wealthy families. They were both rich, arrogant and loved to flaunt their wealth. When Abigail's grandfather died, she inherited a very large, old castle and the couple both decided to move in right away. They set about renovating the castle, and hired a team of builders to perform extensive maintenance work on it.

While the builders were busy cleaning out the basement, they discovered a very large barrel of wine amid all of the clutter. They tried moving it, but found that the barrel was far too heavy for them to lift. One of them had the bright idea that, if they could make the barrel lighter by drinking some of the wine, they would then be able to move it.

Of course the builders were all very quick to agree! After drinking as much as they could, they all found the wine to have a very peculiar taste, but decided to tap the barrel and fill their flasks to the brim to take home for their families to try. Then they carried the barrel upstairs and told Lewis and Abigail of their discovery. Although the barrel was still largely full, it was just light enough for the builders to carry upstairs.

A few weeks later, when all the renovation work had been done, Lewis and Abigail decided to throw a very extravagant housewarming party, and invited all of their family and friends. All of the guests drank glasses of wine filled from the barrel, and by the end of the party, the barrel was almost empty. Everyone had enjoyed the wine, Lewis and Abigail had boasted about their castle, and the housewarming party had been a rousing success.

At the end of the night, when all the guests had gone home, Lewis and Abigail decided to move the near empty barrel back down to the basement. As they were carrying it downstairs, however, they both noticed that it was still decidedly heavy. Lewis decided to investigate further, and so he went off to fetch a hacksaw, and cut off the top of the barrel. However, when both he and his wife looked inside, they were both horrified.

Curled up at the bottom of the barrel was a rotten and decomposed body!

They later found out that it was the corpse of Abigail's grandfather. He had died while abroad and his body had been shipped across in a barrel of wine to help prevent it from decomposing too quickly. However, the barrel had been stored in the basement and not touched - that was, until the married couple moved in.

> I went on a fishing trip about three weeks ago with my friend. As I watched the seagulls pick at his rotting corpse, I knew that we were finally near land.

The Hitchhiker

I was driving down a deserted country road. It was a dark and windy night. The rain was beating down and I had to slow down to negotiate each twist and turn in the road. I listened to the hum of the engine and the squeak of the wipers on the windscreen.

All of a sudden, the headlights picked out a figure standing in the middle of the road. It was a man and he was waving at me. It was a terrible night to be hitchhiking, so I decided to stop and give him a lift.

I pulled up beside the stranger and he opened the car door and jumped inside.

"Thanks!" he said. "The rain started so fast. I didn't have time to take cover".

"You look like you're soaked to the bone" I said, as I switched on the heating. "There, that should dry you off".

"Thank you" said the man.

We drove on through the heavy rain in silence. I looked at the man. His face was thin and pale, and he had hollow, staring eyes. His hair was messy and his clothes were ragged and dirty. Something about him gave me the creeps!

Without asking for permission, the man reached out and turned on the radio.

"My favourite" he said, with a grin. "I love country music. It has a very calming effect".

I smiled and nodded politely.

Just then, the music was interrupted by the voice of the news announcer.

"We bring you the latest news of the dangerous maniac who escaped from the mental asylum earlier today. The police are still searching for this man. He is considered extremely dangerous and has already killed a doctor and a police officer. If you encounter him, you should exercise extreme caution. Motorists are warned to be on their guard. Police believe the maniac will attempt to escape the area by hitching a lift. If you are driving, do not pick up any hitchhikers. I repeat, if you are driving..."

All of a sudden, the stranger leaned over and switched off the radio. I eyed him suspiciously.

"Why did you turn it off?" I asked.

"It's not good listening to stuff like that" replied the man, "especially on a night like this".

Our eyes met and a look of understanding came over his face.

"Wait a second" said the man. "You don't think I'm the escaped maniac, do you?"

"Of course not" I replied, nervously. "You were hitchhiking back there though".

"Look, I swear to you. It's not me" said the man, as he reached into his pocket and pulled out his identification. "My name is Nathan. I'm down on my luck at the moment, but my brother said he has found a job for me working in his factory. I couldn't afford to buy a bus ticket, so that's why I'm hitchhiking".

"Well, you can't blame me for being nervous" I said, "especially on a night like this".

"Don't worry, I understand" said Nathan. "Do I really look like a homicidal maniac though?"

I shook my head.

"Well, let's see if there are any updates" said Nathan, as he switched on the radio again.

The music came on and we waited. The rain was getting heavier and I could barely see the road ahead. Just then, the voice of the news announcer interrupted the music.

"The dead body of a man has been found lying on the side of the highway. Police believe this is another victim of the escaped maniac. His clothes and identification were stolen. The killer's hospital gown was found nearby. Police are warning people to be very careful. The maniac is usually very calm and friendly, but when he gets nervous he will become extremely violent. If you encounter this man, do not try to apprehend him. Just keep him calm and try to call the police. Whatever happens, do not make him nervous..."

Just then, we hit a pothole in the road. The car swerved and skidded into a ditch. I revved the engine and the wheels spun, but no matter what I tried, they couldn't get a grip on the road.

"Maybe we could call a pickup truck" suggested Nathan.

"I don't have a mobile phone" I said. "Do you?"

"No" replied Nathan, as he looked out of the window.

"Hey, look!" said Nathan. "There's a house up there. Maybe they have a phone we can use".

We got out of the car and started climbing up the hill. The rain was lashing down and we were getting drenched. When we came to the house, the lights were off and it looked empty.

Nathan knocked on the door, but there was no answer. I tried the door, and to my surprise, it creaked open.

I followed Nathan into the house and he switched on the lights. Inside, it looked warm and cosy. There was a large fireplace, an expensive looking sofa and a dinner table with plates, knives and forks all set out. I was just glad to be out of the rain. Nathan looked around and grinned at me.

"It looks like there's no phone" he said. "That's too bad".

"Yes, too bad" I said, with a shaky voice.

"What are you so nervous about?" asked Nathan. "Look at you. Your face is pale and your hands are trembling".

I didn't answer.

Then Nathan moved towards me, staring at me with his hollow eyes.

"You still think I'm the escaped maniac, don't you?" asked Nathan, as he chuckled.

"Keep away from me, Nathan!" I shouted, as I backed up against the wall. "Keep away from me!"

"You're afraid of me, aren't you?" asked Nathan, as he laughed and took another step closer.

"I know you want to kill me" I shouted, as I grabbed a knife from the dinner table, "but I'm not going to give you the chance!"

I blacked out for a moment. I don't really know what happened next. It all got a little crazy. When I came around, there was blood everywhere. It was a horrible sight. Nathan was lying on the floor, with his hollow eyes staring up at me. It was either him or me, right?

Just then, I heard a car pull up outside. The front door creaked open and two police officers were standing there. They looked at me, and then they looked at Nathan, as he was lying there in a pool of his own blood.

"That's him!" shouted one of the officers, as they both drew their guns.

"No!" I screamed. "You can't take me back there! I won't go back! I won't go back!"

> After my best friend committed suicide, I started a charity in her honour to combat cyber-bullying. I will admit it took a lot of work to finally push her over the edge, but I'm just so happy that I can now add this charity work to my university applications.

4

Sticky Notes

One evening a young girl called Chloe arrived home from school and found the house empty. Her mother had left a sticky note on the fridge for her. It said that she was out shopping, her father was working late and her two younger brothers were at football practice. So she was alone in the house.

Chloe locked the front door just in case, and then she hung her house keys on a hook, placed her mobile phone on the hallway table and went upstairs to her bedroom to change her clothes.

As she was getting undressed, she saw a sticky note on her bed. She picked up the message and it read "There's someone in the house". She assumed that it was her younger brothers playing a trick on her and immediately crumpled up the note and threw it in the bin.

"Okay, very funny you guys!" she blurted out. "What happened? Did you two miss football practice?"

No one answered.

"Hey, I know you're here! If I find out you two have been through my stuff again, I'm going to kill you both!" she yelled.

No one answered.

Chloe then went downstairs to the kitchen to make a snack for herself. When she opened the fridge door, she discovered another sticky note that read "There's nobody here but you and me". She immediately dropped the note and shouted out "hey guys, this is not funny anymore - stop it!"

No one answered.

Chloe then went to the front door and tried the door knob, but it was securely locked. She turned around to get her house keys, but the hook she had hung them on was empty! Then Chloe glanced down the hallway and noticed that her mobile phone had disappeared from the hallway table. On the table, however, there was another sticky note that read "You're not going anywhere!"

Chloe let out a terrified scream and picked up the home telephone to call the police, but there was no dial tone. She grabbed at the telephone wire only to realise that the wire had been cut!

Chloe then noticed another sticky note by the telephone that read "No phone, no police and no way out!"

Trembling with fear, Chloe ran to the back door of the house. When she tried to turn the handle, she found that it was also locked. Just then, she spotted another sticky note stuck to the back door that read "Look up!" So she looked up only to see her pet rabbit speared and pinned to the ceiling with a kitchen knife.

She screamed in terror and ran to the nearest window. She tried punching and kicking at it, but she couldn't smash the glass. It wouldn't even crack slightly. Then she noticed another sticky note on the window that read "You're not having much luck, are you?"

The frightened Chloe tried to think of what she could do. She needed a knife to defend herself, so she ran into the kitchen - but when she pulled the drawer open, it was empty! All the knives were gone, and in their place was another sticky note that read "Children shouldn't be playing with knives!"

Frightened and terrified, Chloe ran upstairs to her bedroom and locked the door. She checked inside of her wardrobe and underneath her bed, but there was no one there. She breathed a big sigh of relief, but then all of a sudden, her television set turned on by itself. It displayed only loud static, and on the screen she found another sticky note that read "Now I have you exactly where I want you!"

Chloe flew into an immediate panic and started yelling and screaming "help, help, someone help me!" Just then she remembered her computer and quickly sent an e-mail to her best friend. She wrote "Help! This is not a joke! Call the police! There's someone in my house!"

Minutes later she heard the sound of sirens outside the house. The police had arrived and broke down the front door. Two police officers burst into her bedroom and found her cowering in the corner of the room shaking and quivering with fear.

The police searched the entire house from top to bottom and examined every nook and cranny, but they found no one. As the officers were interviewing her, one of them spotted a sticky note attached to Chloe's back. He pulled it off and handed the sticky note to her.

It read "I was this close…"

- One day I arrived home from work. As I lived alone, I started preparing my evening meal in the kitchen. Just then I heard a knock at the door - and heard someone else say "come in!"

5

My Show

I have always felt that things just seemed to work out in my life. Even when I didn't do so well in school, or struggled with losses in my family, everything always ended up working out for me. There was always a silver lining to everything. My family always told me that I was just lucky, and to be thankful for that, but I never felt this way. I didn't believe that anyone could be so lucky.

Take my brother for example. Nothing ever seemed to work out for him. Anything that could go wrong for him would, and anything that could go right for me did. It just can't be a coincidence.

I began to realise that everything in my life was planned. It was like my life was a show, and someone behind the scenes had everything planned out for me no matter what happened. It was like I was the star of the show and set up to succeed, and my brother was just some forgotten sidekick. I truly started to believe this and I had to test my theory.

I started to behave erratically and as unpredictable as I could. I drove different ways to work, just to see if they had the scenery set up. I walked into random stores, just to see if they were real. I made plans, but then cancelled at the very last minute only to do something completely different.

My family and friends told me that they were worried about me. They told me that I didn't seem myself. Perhaps the producers of my show had figured out that I knew what was going on, so they had my family try to bring me back to my normal self. I won't be played like that!

Then, I tried my most daring attempt yet. One night, I got into my car and just began driving. After hours of driving, in any direction, I pulled into a motel for the night and went to sleep happy for the first time in a long time. I truly believed that I had outsmarted the producers this time!

I woke up in the same bed, but I found myself on some sort of studio set with a man sitting next to me in a director's chair.

"Well, look who decided to wake up" said the man. "You gave us quite a fright there, leaving in the middle of the night like that".

The man then revealed a gun that he had been holding and began to polish it.

"You know, we realised you had figured things out a little while back, but decided to let it go" said the man. "You are a clever one, figuring it out the way you did. However, you made one fatal error. The show was never about you. It was always about your brother. You, my friend, were an extra - and now your brother will have to deal with your tragic death this season".

> I never go to sleep, but I keep waking up!

> It wasn't much of a shock to me when the doctor explained that I have multiple personality disorder. The shock was when I learned that I wasn't the original personality!

The Accident

One evening a husband and wife were travelling by car through the countryside when, in the distance, they could see a woman in the middle of the road waving frantically.

The wife told her husband to keep on driving for fear that it may be dangerous or some kind of trap. As they got closer the husband slowed down and, not seeing any evidence of a trap, stopped the car to see what kind of assistance the woman needed.

When they got out of the car they noticed that the woman had cuts and bruises on her face and arms. They both asked the woman if she needed any assistance.

The woman ran over frantically begging for their help, telling them that she had been in a car accident and both her husband and daughter, a newborn baby, were still inside the car, which had come to rest at the bottom of a deep ditch. She told them that her husband was already dead, but that her baby still seemed to be alive and begged for them to help rescue her!

The husband decided to make his way down the ditch to see if he could rescue the baby, while his wife stayed with the poor woman by the side of the road, who was clearly distressed and in shock, and try to calm her down.

When he finally got down to the wreckage he saw the baby still sitting in the back seat, so he loosened her seat belt and pulled her from the mangled wreck of a car. When he got back to the roadside holding the baby his wife was there looking for him, but the mother of the baby was nowhere to be seen. His wife told him that she had followed him down to the car, just in case he needed any assistance with the baby. Fearing for the safety of the woman, the husband then went back down to look for the mother of the baby.

When the husband got back down to the wreckage, he noticed that there were two people sitting in the front seats of the car who were clearly dead, but the passenger was unmistakeably the woman who had flagged them down.

> The taxi driver wasn't very chatty, so I decided to check my mobile phone. At that moment I received a text message saying "This is your taxi driver - I'm waiting outside".

The Tourist

Holly had just finished studying at university, and before she embarked on her career as an interior designer, she decided to take a year out travelling abroad. She was only 23 years old and always wanted the experience of travelling to more obscure and exotic places. She wanted a trip that was going to be exciting and new, and that offered mountains, forests and unusual cultures to explore.

So Holly decided to go backpacking for a few months and just see where it took her. She was looking forward to the freedom of travelling through remote areas and meeting new people along the way.

When her plane arrived at her first destination, the only luggage she had with her was the small backpack she was carrying on her back. However, Holly didn't want to stay for very long in the hustle and bustle of the city, as she was eager to explore the hills and the valleys of the vast country.

Holly decided that she was going to turn this little backpacking trip into a much more interesting adventure. So she decided to jump on a bus, without having any idea where it was going. Not knowing the destination made it feel like she was taking a mystery tour around the country. Every time the bus reached the end of the line, she would jump off and randomly catch another bus, never knowing or caring where it would take her.

After a few weeks, she found herself travelling around some of the most remote regions of the country. These were areas that tourists rarely visited. Holly was delighted to be passing through all these small villages and having the opportunity to see how these people really lived.

One day, she found herself travelling on yet another bus, and passing through yet another remote area. When the bus set off it was virtually empty, but after five or six stops a large crowd of people had got on and it was filled to capacity.

After a while, she noticed that many of the other passengers kept looking at her strangely. Holly also thought it was odd that they chose to stand instead of sitting down in the vacant seat next to her.

At the next stop a handsome young man boarded the bus. He looked around, and when he saw the young backpacker his eyes suddenly grew wide with shock. When he hurried down the aisle and sat down right beside her, Holly was surprised.

Suddenly, the man nudged her and whispered "do you know where you are going?"

"I have no idea" replied Holly, with a smile. "I'm just backpacking around the country. I got on this bus without looking at the destination".

"Well I must warn you that you are in grave danger" said the man.

"Why?" asked Holly.

"The next stop is the end of the line" replied the man. "It is a village that has an awful reputation. The people who live there are cannibals, and they prey on tourists who are lost!"

Holly couldn't believe what the man was saying. At first she thought that he must be joking, but when she looked at his face, she could see that he was very serious!

"Surely you can't expect me to believe that?" asked Holly.

"What I am telling you is the truth" replied the man. "If you are wise, you will take heed of what I tell you. Everyone in this area has heard the horrible tales of what goes on in that village. It is commonly called 'The Man-Eating Village!'"

The man's words shocked Holly to her very core. She found herself lost for words!

"If you don't believe me, just look around you" said the man. "Almost all of the passengers on this bus are from that village".

Holly looked up and suddenly realised that almost all of the other passengers were staring at her and licking their lips.

"When the bus reaches the end of the line, you will be in their territory" said the man. "No one will be able to save you then. They will take hold of you and eat you alive!"

Holly broke out into a cold sweat. She could see the murderous look in the eyes of the salivating passengers. She had to escape before the bus reached the village.

Just then, Holly felt the bus begin to slow down as it ascended a steep mountain road.

"This is our chance" said the man. "Let's go!"

The man grabbed Holly by the hand and they both ran down the aisle towards the back of the bus before the other passengers had the chance to react. The man pulled the handle on the emergency exit and then jumped out. Holly was right behind him and leaped through the narrow opening.

She crashed onto the dirt road and rolled over, before picking herself up. She saw the man jump across a ditch and run off, so she followed him, running just as fast as she could!

They escaped into the mountain, as the angry calls of the other passengers echoed behind them. Holly fled for her life, scrambling up the steep mountain slope, desperate to evade the hungry cannibals who were pursuing her.

Eventually, the passengers gave up the chase and returned to the bus. Holly was exhausted, but she was overjoyed that she had managed to escape their ravenous clutches.

As she lay on a large rock, trying to catch her breath, she heard the man laughing softly to himself.

"You tourists are always so trusting" said the man, as he stared at her licking his lips.

- "It would appear you have discovered an entirely new kind of termite" said the doctor, while staring inquisitively at my x-rays. "This would also explain the aching you've been feeling in your bones".

8

The Werewolf

A priest from a thriving town was travelling to a small village on business for the church. The priest's journey across the countryside was long and arduous, and as night grew near, he was forced to stop overnight at an old and largely deserted motel that was reputed to be haunted.

During the night, the priest heard a clawing and scratching noise outside of his door. When he went out to investigate, he was attacked by a wolf!

He was bitten quite severely, and just as he thought the wolf was about to finish him off, the cross hanging around his neck became exposed. The wolf suddenly ceased its attack and merely stood over him, staring into his eyes. Then, inexplicably, it ran off into the woods, leaving him lying on the ground and bleeding badly from his wounds.

The next day, he managed to make his way to the village, where he was treated by the local doctor. With good medical care, his wounds soon healed and he was back to work in no time. The priest was re-energised and tackled his church duties with renewed vigour. He inspired the villagers and helped them to build a new church. The faith of the villagers was strengthened and every day the church was packed with his followers.

There were still problems in the village, however, as every full moon, someone in the village was either found dead, or went missing under mysterious circumstances. People said that they had seen a creature stalking the village at night - a creature that walked like a man, but whose body was covered in fur and bore the head of a wolf. There was talk of a curse on the village, and many believed that a werewolf was stalking them and picking them off one by one.

The priest began to wonder why the village had been cursed with these horrible murders and disappearances, and it seemed like there was no end to it.

One night, during a full moon, the villagers decided that they had to catch and kill the werewolf that was plaguing their village once and for all. They set a trap by tying the most beautiful girl in the village to a tree and using her as bait to lure the werewolf. High above the girl, in the branches of the tree, they rigged a trap to catch the wolf. Then, they hid in the bushes and waited.

Soon, they heard a crashing noise coming through the forest and suddenly, the werewolf appeared. As it made its way towards the terrified young girl, the villagers cut the ropes that were tied to the tree and a huge cage came crashing down on top of the wolf, trapping it behind the heavy iron bars.

The jubilant villagers rushed out from their hiding places and drove long spears into the body of the werewolf. As the murderous beast collapsed to the floor of the cage, the people watched as its hairy body rippled and changed.

Gradually, the creature changed from wolf to man, as the life ebbed from its body. The villagers fell to their knees and began to weep when they realised that they had killed their beloved priest.

➢ One of two armed police officers suddenly collapsed and became unresponsive. The other police officer called the emergency services in a panic and said "my friend is dead, what should I do?" The operator replied "calm down, let's make sure he's really dead first?" There was a short pause before a sudden, loud gunshot. "Right, he's dead - now what?" said the police officer.

9

The Plan

On Friday I came up with the perfect plan. Craig was my best friend outside of work, but at the office we worked in different departments and on different floors, so no one ever saw us together. No one knew that we were friends.

Craig worked on the ground floor. At least he used to. He had recently been sacked for 'poor performance'. The claims of a bad attitude against him didn't help, but I know his co-workers just didn't like it when he stood up for himself. He really needed this job, and I know Craig is a good person, but I knew that he was the vengeful type too.

I was still employed there, just sitting up on the 1st floor every day working on the computer and taking telephone calls. I needed the job more than Craig did, but things weren't going well for me either. My performance was also deemed to be 'poor', and I had a few disagreements with my work colleagues too. It's alright for them to question your work and your work ethic, but as soon as you rightfully justify yourself, you are the disruptive one!

There were lots of cliques in that place! Craig and I were both good, hard-working people, but we hated our co-workers - and most of all, our bosses! I didn't think I would be too far behind Craig out of the door.

So I came up with the perfect plan. I had all weekend to perfect the plan with Craig, and we would carry out the plan on Monday.

Our office block had only the ground and first floor, with no more than eight or nine employees on each. About 10am on Monday morning everyone would be in the office and sitting at their desks working. Craig would pull up in his car around the back of the building. Fortunately, I could see the back of the building from my window and there were no cameras there. When I saw him arrive, I would place a large, yellow folder up against the window. That was my signal to him that we were good to go!

Then Craig would walk around to the main entrance and burst into the building, hidden behind a mask, and just start shooting. He and his family all had guns for 'home defence', so in the perfect act of revenge and vengeance, he would storm into the building and just start shooting.

Craig would quickly work his way around the ground floor and up to the 1st floor. My floor!

Then I would take the gun from Craig, and the 1st floor would be mine! All those people who questioned my work ethic, doubted me and told me that my performance was 'poor'. Of course I couldn't possibly forget my boss - I think I will save him for last!

Once we were done, Craig would escape out of the back emergency exit and flee in his car, and I would then call the police, claiming that I had just cowered in a corner and hid the whole time. We knew the building so well and we talked through our plan in great detail, so we felt sure that we had a good chance of pulling it off. Our lives were pretty much going from one disaster to another anyway, so we both had very little to lose!

So that was the plan. Craig had already been sacked. He was going to lose his house, his girlfriend would undoubtedly leave him and his life was going down the drain. I could see his life unravelling as a reflection of what was to come for me.

So Monday morning came, and I was feeling quite good about the plan. I wasn't nervous at all actually. As 10am approached, I looked out of the window and saw Craig approach in his car around the back of the building and park up. I looked around me and everyone was quiet and just getting on with their work, so I propped the yellow folder up against the window as a signal to Craig. Almost immediately I saw Craig getting out of his car, with his mask already on, and march with purpose towards the main entrance.

Suddenly, I heard the shots going off. Bang! Bang! Bang! That's when the screaming started. Almost as quickly as the screaming had started, it stopped. I just sat there looking around and pretending to look confused, just as everyone else did, but I knew exactly what was happening. It was quite a rush!

It was no more than a minute before Craig had arrived at the 1st floor. That was the moment when I stood up, walked over to Craig and took the gun from him - and then I turned around and just started shooting. Bang! Bang! Bang! What a beautiful moment. I didn't mess around. I spared no one. I even had the pleasure of bursting into my boss's office, and while he was cowering under his desk, just started shooting. Thankfully, Craig had brought plenty of ammunition!

Well, that was it. Mission accomplished! Everyone in the building was dead, including Craig's boss and my boss. Craig and I had taken revenge on all our horrible co-workers and bosses. Now all we had to do was for Craig to escape through the emergency exit, and then shortly after, for me to call the police while sounding desperately frantic and distressed.

However, there was just one piece of the plan left. A tiny little detail that I had forgot to tell Craig about.

That was the part where I shot Craig, and then claimed to have wrestled the gun from him and shot him before he had the opportunity to kill me and get away - and that's exactly what I did!

I was deemed a hero for stopping and shooting the vengeful ex-employee, and was celebrated within both my company and the local community. I was even promoted to a higher paid job in one of the company's other office blocks.

It was indeed the perfect plan.

> "Don't move, it's right behind you!" said my sister, as she stood right in front of me. I slowly turned around, only to see my sister - the same sister - who said "don't move, it's right behind you!"

10

Seaweed

My grandmother grew up in the slums of a very rough neighbourhood. Her family lived in a small house near the harbour, and one of her earliest memories was of a particularly hot summer when, seeking respite from the heat, she and her sister discovered a seldom-used section of pathway near an abandoned warehouse.

Every night, for several weeks, she and her sister would make their way down to the docks and sit together on the edge of the pier as the sun went down.

My grandmother recalled vividly, and quite fondly, the feel of the seaweed between her toes as she and her sister dangled their feet into the murky water below.

It wasn't until years later, when she returned to the pier, that she found out the warehouse had been demolished. Feeling curious, she made an enquiry with the local Department of Planning and Development. Apparently, the warehouse had been owned and used for a time by a group of criminals, who were using it as a base of operation for a local prostitution racket. It had only been uncovered when an associate began 'disposing' of rival prostitutes by fitting them with concrete shoes and dumping them into the harbour.

Investigating officers had recovered dozens of bodies from just beneath the surface of the water by the secluded pier. How had the bodies been discovered? Well, a passing fisherman spotted the hair of the victims floating near the surface of the water, just like seaweed.

> I can hear exactly one year into the future. Today, the noise stopped!

> My bullies surrounded me sneering and taunting me as they yanked my cap off. I cried and screamed but they didn't stop as they moved on to my other knee.

11

The Phone Booth

There were two teenage girls called Rebecca and Sharon who both shared an interest in anything paranormal. Whenever they met, they would always have a new scary ghost story or a spooky urban legend to share with each other.

One day, Sharon was browsing the internet on her computer when she came across a website that had a lot of urban legends. She read a story about a certain suspension bridge that was located close to where she lived. The website had plenty of pictures of the bridge and the surrounding area. As she read the legend associated with the bridge, Sharon knew that Rebecca would be very interested.

The next time she saw Rebecca, she told her about the bridge. It was an old suspension bridge that crossed over a very deep gorge. For some inexplicable reason, it was known to be a spot notorious for suicides. Every year, around 20 to 30 people would throw themselves off that bridge and plunge to their deaths. No one could explain why. Some people said that the bridge was haunted by the ghosts of the people who had committed suicide there.

When Rebecca went home that evening, she decided that she had to check out the bridge. She desperately wanted to see a ghost! So that very night, she set out for the mountains where the bridge was located. It took her about half an hour to get there.

It was just after midnight when she arrived at the bridge, and there was not a single person around. It was eerily dark and deathly quiet there, with only the moonlight to cast shadows across the bridge. The atmosphere was so spooky and ominous that it sent a chill down Rebecca's spine.

"Wow! This place is creepy" muttered Rebecca to herself, as she cautiously walked to the edge of the gorge and peered down into its depths. She began to think of all the people who had thrown themselves down into the blackness. The thought of it made her hair stand on end.

It was so fascinating that she felt compelled to tell her friend Sharon about it, so she pulled out her mobile phone to call her. However, since she was high up in the mountains, she couldn't get any reception on her phone.

Looking around, Rebecca noticed a solitary phone booth standing nearby. She walked over to it, stepped inside and put some coins in the slot before dialling Sharon's number.

"Hello Sharon, you'll never guess where I am right now?" said Rebecca. "I'm at the suspension bridge you told me about. The view is amazing! You've got to come up here and see it sometime".

"Yeah, I'd like to" said Sharon. "I saw all the pictures on the website. Wait a minute - what number are you calling me from?"

"Oh, I couldn't get any reception on my mobile phone, so I'm calling from the payphone up here" replied Rebecca.

Sharon was confused.

"Payphone?" said Sharon. "There's no payphone up there. I would have seen it in the pictures".

"What are you talking about?" said Rebecca. "I'm standing in the phone booth right at the entrance to the bridge. Hold on, I'd better go. There's a line of people outside waiting to use the phone. I'll call you when I get home".

As soon as Rebecca said that, Sharon shouted "No! Rebecca, don't get out of the phone booth! I know that place - I'll be right there in 30 minutes. Whatever you do, don't move!"

"What's wrong?" asked Rebecca.

"Just promise me you'll stay right where you are and don't move an inch, okay?" replied Sharon. "I'll be right there!"

When Sharon hung up the phone, Rebecca felt a wave of fear envelop her. She stood in the phone booth and kept the phone receiver pressed to her ear. Looking over her shoulder, she saw a line of people standing outside the phone booth silently watching her. Their blank expressions and cold stares sent a shiver down her spine.

Half an hour later, when Sharon arrived at the suspension bridge, she found Rebecca standing on the very edge of the bridge overlooking the gorge.

She was holding her mobile phone to her ear. There was no phone booth and no line of people waiting to use the phone.

As Sharon rushed towards her friend, Rebecca saw her coming - and at that moment she stepped out of the phone booth.

> I dialled 'last caller' to tell the guy who keeps calling my mobile phone all night, and threatening to kill me, to leave me alone. My blood ran cold when I heard the telephone ringing upstairs.

The Maid

There was a very wealthy man who was married to a woman much younger than himself. He often suspected that she might be having an affair, but he could never be truly sure.

One day, when he was away on a business trip, he called his house to check up on her. The phone was answered by a female voice that he didn't recognise.

"Who are you?" asked the man.

"I'm the maid" replied the woman.

"What? We don't have a maid?" asked the man.

"The lady of the house just hired me this morning" replied the maid.

"Well, I'm the gentleman of the house" he said. "Can you put my wife on the phone?"

"I don't think I can" replied the maid.

"Why? Where is she?" asked the man.

"She's upstairs in her bedroom with a man" replied the maid. "I thought he was her husband!"

When he heard this, the man flew into a rage!

In a growling voice, he asked the maid "right, how would you like to make £100,000?"

The maid paused and thought for a moment, before replying "that's an awful lot of money - what would you want me to do?"

The man replied "I want you to go to the gun safe, and I want you to take one of my guns, load it up, and then go upstairs and shoot that no-good wife of mine, and the stupid guy she's been having an affair with!"

The maid thought about it, and after a long pause, she finally said "alright, I'll do it!"

The man heard the sound of the maid placing the phone down on the table. He then heard her footsteps as she walked away from the phone. A few minutes later, he heard two distinct screams, immediately followed by the sound of six loud gunshots! There was a long silence, before he heard footsteps approaching and the maid pick up the phone.

"Okay, it's done" she said, nervously. "What shall I do with the bodies?"

"Just throw them in conservatory for now" replied the man. "I'll see to them when I arrive home".

"Conservatory?" asked the maid, "but you don't have a conservatory?"

There was a long, awkward silence, before the man eventually replied "oh, I'm very sorry, I must have dialled the wrong number" and hung up.

➢ I always kiss my husband and two children goodnight before I go to sleep. When I wake up, I'm in a padded room and the nurse tells me it was all just a dream.

Wallpaper

My boyfriend and I bought a new house together, except that it wasn't really that new. It was an old, abandoned house that needed much renovation work to make it inhabitable again. It was our project though, and something that we were both eager and excited to get started on.

My boyfriend was in charge of the construction element of the house - refitting the kitchen for example. I was taking care of the decoration, which started with me having to remove all the beige, blotchy wallpaper from the walls.

The previous owner has papered every wall and ceiling with the same beige, blotchy wallpaper. Removing it all was a long and painstaking job, but we took regular tea breaks to refresh our focus.

Removing the wallpaper was oddly satisfying though. The best feeling was when you got a long peel and a big strip of wallpaper came off. As tedious as the work was, I made a game of it by trying to peel off the longest piece of wallpaper I could before it ripped.

Under the paper, on the bare walls and ceiling, I sporadically found a person's name and a date written down. Clearly, as this was an old house, many of the previous occupants had written the old 'such and such was here' down to forever engrain their name into the house.

One night curiosity got the better of me, and so I searched one of the names on my computer. I was shocked to discover that the person was in fact a missing person, and the date written down matched the date that they had disappeared!

The next day I made a list of all the names I could find, and the dates that were written alongside them. Sure enough, each name was for a missing person with matching dates.

Of course we notified the police, who sent out a crime scene investigation team.

I overheard a couple of investigators talking and one of them saying "yeah, it's human".

"Human?" I asked. "What's human?"

"Well lady" replied one of the investigators, "the material you have been removing from the walls is not wallpaper".

➢ For my last wish, I wished for my ex husband to be alive again. I stood over his grave and smiled, imagining him screaming and clawing at his coffin lid - just as he did the two previous times I wished him back.

14

Natural Habitat

When Christopher touched down on the planet's surface, it was daylight. Looking out the window of his space capsule, he could see the two suns, and there were also five moons orbiting in the sky.

The sensors indicated that the atmosphere of the planet was breathable, so Christopher put on his spacesuit, opened the airlock and cautiously exited the capsule.

He seemed to have landed in a desert area, where mountains of sand stretched as far as the eye could see, and everything was an angry shade of red. He slowly took off his helmet and inhaled a deep breath of air.

That was when he noticed it - the alien craft on the horizon.

Over the mountains of sand, it hovered, coming closer and closer by the second. The craft landed nearby and a hatch opened. Three humanoid figures stepped out. They walked on two legs, and their bodies were shaped much like humans. However, that's where the similarities ended.

They were much taller, and their skin was a sickly shade of green. Their limbs were long and skinny. Their heads were large and bulbous. They had no ears, no noses and tiny, thin mouths without lips. They had strange, shiny black eyes that almost seemed like mirrors.

As he watched the aliens approach, Christopher was careful not to make any sudden movements. He didn't want to scare them off! When they drew near, he waved at them, attempting a friendly gesture. He then extended his hand. The aliens eyed him curiously, but kept their distance.

"My name is Christopher" he said. "I come from planet Earth. I come in peace".

The aliens smiled at him and nodded. They spoke to each other in a curious language of clicks and squeaks. For a while, Christopher tried clumsily to communicate with them. It seemed obvious that they understood him, but he could not understand them.

They beckoned to him and gestured towards their space craft. They wanted him to follow them. As soon as he boarded the craft, the hatch closed behind him and they took off.

The aliens brought him to their city. They led him to a huge and very important looking building, where he followed them down the long halls and corridors until they came to a room.

As soon as they stepped inside the room, he was struck by how familiar it looked. The interior was almost an exact replica of a typical house on Earth. There was a table and chair, a bed and a wardrobe. One wall of the room was covered by long blue curtains.

One of the aliens left and when it came back, it was holding a tray. It set the tray down on the table and gestured for Christopher to sit. He obeyed, and when he lifted the lid on the tray, he was shocked to see a plate containing food. It was a dinner, just like a typical dinner he would have eaten on Earth.

Christopher was impressed by the lengths the aliens had gone to, and all that they had done, to make him feel at home.

The aliens then turned and left, and he heard a distinct click as the door locked behind them. Christopher was hungry, so he picked up the knife and fork and began eating his dinner. As he was eating his dinner, he contemplated his experience, and all that he had to report back on his return to Earth.

Then, he began to hear a low buzzing sound, and the curtains on the wall drew back slowly. Through the window, he could see hundreds, if not thousands, of aliens outside. They were all just gathered there, staring at him. Obviously word had spread of his visit to the planet, and many of the alien population just wanted to get a good look at the visitor from another planet. So Christopher stood up, walked towards the window and waved towards the gathering crowd.

That's when he noticed the bars on the windows - and the sign, that read 'Earth creature in its natural habitat'.

> "I would literally give anything to spend just one more day with my deceased wife" I muttered to myself. As my still deceased wife appeared

sitting upright on the sofa, I saw my only son disappear as if he had never existed.

15

The Best of Friends

The three of us grew up together. We were the best of friends. "Best friends until the end!" is what we always said. I was always the quiet one, Matthew was the sensitive one and Simon was the wild one. Things were always interesting with Simon around, but he had a really bad gambling habit. It was like an addiction - he just couldn't stop himself!

Poker was his game, and he played for high stakes. The problem was he was on a losing streak. He borrowed money left, right and centre, but he just kept on losing! Pretty soon he found himself in way over his head. He owed a whole lot of money to some very bad people. "£50,000" he told us - and if he didn't pay them, they would kill him!

He confided in us and explained the dire situation he was in - after all, Matthew and I were his best friends. When he came to see us, he broke down sobbing. He desperately needed our help. "Best friends until the end" we said, so we agreed to help him in any way that we could.

Simon had it all planned out. He said that he had been watching the bank for almost a month now. We were going to go in there wearing masks and take out the two security cameras with spray paint. Then we would hold the place up! The safe would be locked on a timer of course, but there would be enough money in the service desk drawers for sure. We would walk out with at least £70,000 he told us, which was more than enough to cover Simon's debts, and the rest would be split between Matthew and me.

So we put the plan into action and Simon began driving us to a street just around the corner from the bank. We never made it to the bank, however, as while we were making our way there, a van screeched to a halt right in front of us and five armed men got out. They kidnapped us at gunpoint and bundled us into the back of their van. We lay there on the floor of the van as they tied our hands and our feet really tight.

Simon, however, looked back at us from the car driver's seat and shouted "sorry guys, but the truth is I need a lot more than £50,000, and the organ market is really booming these days!"

> My boyfriend finally stopped smoking. I hate it when I burn the dinner!

> Something on the beach sliced my foot open as I was walking across the sand. I didn't panic - that was until I felt something slither inside of the cut.

16

The Photographer

A friend of mine is a young and very ambitious nature photographer. She loves to go out into the wilderness and take pictures of all sorts of animals, plants and trees. A few months ago she decided to spend a whole day taking photos in a remote part of the forest. It meant that she would have to camp out for the night all alone in the woods.

She was really looking forward to all the amazing photo opportunities she would find with all the interesting trees, plants and wildlife in that area. It would certainly make a welcome addition to her portfolio. She was not afraid to be alone during the night because she had camped out on her own many times before.

She arrived and pitched her tent in the middle of a small clearing, and spent the whole day taking photographs. By the end of the day, when she finally settled down to sleep in the tent, she had taken over 300 photographs on her digital camera.

The next day when she was back at home, and on her computer scrolling through all the photos she had taken, she noticed something very strange. What she saw in those photographs has haunted her ever since. In fact, she is still recovering from the trauma of it to this very day.

You see, all the pictures were very normal and accounted for, except for the very last one. It was of her asleep in the tent in the middle of the night!

➤ A smile of relief washed across his face, even with his arm swallowed nearly to the elbow by the drain. "I think I can feel your ring!" he said. I smiled too and said "oh, that's great - and I know about your affair!" as I flipped the disposal switch.

17

The Light

There were two girls called Emma and Danielle who were the best of friends in school. When they both went to university, they decided to live together and become housemates.

One night, they were staying up late in Danielle's room trying to do some last-minute studying for the exam that was scheduled for the following morning.

Danielle was quite lazy, so she decided to give up on studying and went to bed early. Emma was a hard worker, so she returned to her room and decided to stay up late, because she wanted to do well in the exam.

During the night, Emma remembered that one of the books she needed was in Danielle's room. She didn't want to wake her housemate by turning on the light, so she sneaked into her room and started rummaging around in the dark looking for the book she needed.

Emma heard some heavy breathing, groaning and tossing and turning coming from Danielle's bed. She was obviously having a bad dream - perhaps about failing the exam! Still, just to make sure that Danielle was alright, Emma whispered her name to see if she was awake.

There was no answer.

Then Emma heard distinct movement coming from where Danielle was sleeping. Again, Emma whispered "can I turn on the light?"

There was no answer.

Emma then said in a more stern voice "can I turn on the light? I really need to find something".

There was no answer.

Emma sighed in frustration and continued searching in the dark for the book she needed. Eventually, when she found the book she was looking for, she took the book and felt her way through the darkness towards the door.

Emma stayed up all night studying, and in the morning she raced down to the exam hall to take her exam. She noticed, however, that Danielle never turned up to take the exam.

Emma was worried about her friend, so when she arrived back home, she rushed upstairs and knocked on Danielle's door.

There was no answer.

Emma began to feel quite anxious at this point, so she opened the door and noticed that the room was still in darkness because the curtains were still closed. Emma turned on the bedroom light and was met with the most horrible sight she had ever seen.

Danielle was sprawled across her bed, completely motionless, and lying in a pool of her own blood. She had been brutally murdered! Then Emma turned around and saw something that chilled her to the bone.

Written in blood across the wall behind her were the words "Aren't you glad you didn't turn on the light, Emma?"

> Although their marriage was on the rocks, their only daughter was shocked to arrive home to a suicide note resting on the living room table. She failed to hear the footsteps creeping up behind her as she noticed that the name signed at the bottom of the note - was hers!

18

The Patient

There was a young man called Neil who was in hospital for a few weeks after recovering from an operation. The room he was staying in was very large, and he shared it with a number of other patients. One of the other patients was a tall, thin man with pale skin, hollow eyes and sunken cheeks.

The man was behaving quite strangely, and it made Neil feel anxious and nervous to be around him. At night, when everyone was asleep, the man would quietly sneak out of the room and go somewhere. In the early hours of the morning, he would come back and silently get back into bed as if nothing had happened.

This went on night after night, and the man's behaviour was so suspicious that it had Neil wondering what he was up to.

One night Neil just couldn't get to sleep. As he lay there awake, he noticed the man getting out of bed and leaving the room without making a sound. Driven by curiosity, he decided to follow him.

The man walked down the stairs, out of a side door and left the hospital grounds. Neil stayed a safe distance behind him, and the man seemed to have no idea that he was being followed.

When he came to the nearby cemetery, the man went inside. Neil thought that it was very odd for someone to visit the cemetery in the middle of the night, but he was curious to see what the man was up to, so he followed him inside.

The man slowly made his way through the cemetery, and eventually stopped in front of one of the graves. Neil made sure to stay in the shadows, moving silently and hiding behind the gravestones. He saw the man crouch down, but Neil was too far away to see what he was doing. Carefully, he crawled closer to get a better view.

What he saw filled him with horror! The man was digging up a grave with his bare hands and pulling out the remains. Then, in the moonlight, he picked up the bones and began chewing and gnawing on them, while stripping and consuming whatever flesh remained.

Neil was so terrified by what he saw that he instinctively let out a gasp!

At that moment the man suddenly stopped chewing, looked around and stayed very still. He seemed to sense that he was being watched.

Neil grew very scared, so he turned around and ran. He ran straight back to the hospital, up the stairs and hurried back to his room. Jumping into his bed, he pulled the covers over himself and pretended to be asleep.

A short time later, the man came back to the room. Neil was in a panic, but he kept his eyes closed and tried to stay calm. He could hear footsteps moving around the room.

When Neil opened one eye to take a peek, he could see that the man was going from one bed to another, and he seemed to be looking in the face of each patient as they slept. Neil could hear him muttering something under his breath, but he couldn't make out what he was saying.

He waited and waited as the footsteps came closer and closer. Neil was trying to keep perfectly still.

Eventually the man arrived at his bed.

The man leaned in close, put his hands on Neil's chest and said "one, two, three… your heart is beating very fast, so you're the one who saw me!"

➤ My son told me that his mirror image was threatening to replace him in the real world. I thought he was just imagining things, until today when I saw my right handed son using his left hand to write.

19

The Waiter

When my mother was young she went out on a blind date. Her date took her to a restaurant, and although he was nice enough, she just didn't find him that interesting. Halfway through the meal she was so bored that she was already thinking of excuses to leave early! The waiter who was serving their table could tell that she was bored, and kept smiling and winking at her.

While my mother's date was using the washroom, the waiter approached her and asked if she was alright. She explained that she was on a blind date, but that she wasn't really having much fun.

It turned out that the waiter was just about to finish his shift, so he offered to give her a lift home, if she waited another ten minutes. She considered his offer briefly and was just about to say yes, but at that very moment her date arrived back from the washroom - so she shook her head, smiled at the waiter and said "no thanks".

My mother and her date finished their meals, and he then drove her home.

The very next night my mother just happened to be watching the evening news. There was a newsflash saying that a woman had been found murdered behind a restaurant the night before. She suddenly realised that it was the very same restaurant from where she had been with her blind date!

Then they said that the police had already caught the killer, and a picture flashed up on the screen. It was the waiter.

Her blind date had unwittingly saved her life by returning from the washroom just in time.

➤ I grabbed my husband's arm tightly as we walked through the haunted house. By the time we got out he was nowhere to be found, but I was still holding his arm.

Hide and Seek

A young couple decided that they would both get married after studying at university. The father of the bride was very wealthy and was able to afford a very big wedding for them. The wedding was beautiful, and afterwards they had a big reception in a large, old building where everyone got very drunk. The bride and groom's family and friends laughed, danced and sang long into the night.

When there were only about ten people left, the groom decided that they should all play a game of hide and seek. Everyone agreed and the groom volunteered to be the one to search for the group - so while he covered his eyes and counted to 60, they all ran to find hiding spots.

After about 20 minutes everyone had been found, except for the bride. The remaining guests searched everywhere - they called out her name and looked everywhere trying to find her, but they couldn't find a single trace of her! A few hours later everyone gave up the search and the guests went home. The groom was left feeling upset and rather furious, thinking that the bride was playing some sort of terrible trick on him.

As the weeks passed, the heartbroken groom, having already filed a missing persons report, gave up looking for her. He concluded that she must have had second thoughts about the wedding and decided to leave him. Eventually, he accepted this and moved on with his life.

About 20 years later a cleaning lady was busy tidying the large, old building where the reception had been held. She happened to be in the attic when she noticed a large, dusty old trunk just lying on the floor in the corner of the room. She dusted it off and, out of sheer curiosity, decided to open it. She screamed at the top of her voice and immediately ran out of the building to call the police.

Apparently the bride had decided to hide in the trunk for the game of hide and seek. When she climbed in, the lid had fallen and locked her inside. The trunk was solid and the attic was far up in the building, so neither could she break her way out nor anyone hear her screams.

The bride was found still dressed in her bridal gown, with her wedding ring still placed on her bony finger. It is unknown whether the bride had suffocated or starved to death, but she was found completely decomposed and with her mouth hanging open in silent scream.

- I used to be considered the evil twin, but now I'm considered an only child.

- After I died, I felt myself rise and float away from my body. I look down to see my lifeless body just lying there - and then, it woke up!

21

The Railway Crossing

A man was driving home from work one evening when he came to a railway crossing. The traffic lights had turned to red, so he stopped the car in front of the tracks. He heard the bell ringing and saw the barrier slowly coming down.

As he glanced to his left, he noticed a teenage schoolgirl hurrying down the pavement at the side of the road. When she saw the barrier coming down she started running, trying to cross the tracks before the train came.

Halfway across the railway tracks, the girl suddenly stopped. Her foot had become caught in the gap between the wooden slats and the metal rail. The train was fast approaching, and the man watched in horror as the girl tried desperately to free herself.

The man jumped out of his car and ran over to the barrier. He began waving his hands and shouting in a desperate attempt to warn the train driver. It was no use. The girl couldn't free herself and she was screaming "help me, I don't want to die!"

The man turned away and hid his eyes as the train thundered through the intersection. He cringed as he heard the girl's scream suddenly cut off by the deafening 'clack clack' of the train on the tracks.

As the train roared off into the distance, he gingerly opened his eyes and forced himself to look. He braced himself for the terrible sight he was expecting to see, but the railway tracks were completely empty.

There was no sign of the girl's mangled body.

There was no blood at all.

He looked around while wondering what had happened to her.

"Where could she be? Did she manage to free herself in time?" he thought to himself.

Just then, he noticed a small, metal plaque on the wall between the barrier and the railway tracks. It was covered in dirt, had gone very rusty and was partly hidden by weeds. It appeared like it had been there for years, if not decades.

The plaque read 'In loving memory of our darling daughter. May she Rest in Peace'.

> I've always had the supernatural ability to know exactly where someone is just by looking at a picture of them. So it pains me to tell the wife of a missing husband that her husband is in several different places.

22

False Teeth

There was an old woman who found herself homeless. Every night she would sleep in an alley, and during the day, she would wander around the city rooting through rubbish bins looking for something to eat. The old woman had never taken care of her teeth and they had all fallen out many years ago. So every time she ate something she had to mush the food up with her gums.

One night, as she was doing her rounds and searching through rubbish bins for food, she spotted something that appeared rather unusual lying on the ground. She stooped down to take a closer look and lying there in a pool of blood was a pair of false teeth.

Unable to believe her luck, she picked up the false teeth and wiped them down with an old rag. After looking over them, she stuck them in her mouth to try them out. They were a perfect fit! The old woman wanted to try them out, so she retrieved some leftover pizza from one of the rubbish bins and bit into it. The false teeth worked just perfectly!

After a while the old woman began to feel really hungry. She rooted through more rubbish bins and found all sorts of discarded food from takeaways and people's leftovers - most of it a little old and mouldy, but satisfying none-the-less. Stuffing them all into her mouth, however, she found that the more she ate the more hungry she became.

It wasn't long before the old woman had eaten everything that she could find discarded in the rubbish bins. Then she spotted a rat rummaging through some of the rubbish lying on the ground. So she chased it down the alley and when she caught up with it, she just rammed it straight into her mouth, chewed it up and swallowed it down - tail and all!

A young man on a bicycle then came riding by. The old woman grabbed him and chomped on him until he was all gone. She even ate his bicycle for dessert, but her hunger was still not satisfied!

A homeless man was sleeping in a doorway - she ate him before he even had the chance to wake up!

Then when a woman stopped at a red light in her car, the old woman pulled her out through the window and gobbled her down as well.

A short time later a policeman was walking his daily route when he saw the old woman gnawing on a lamp post. He walked up to her and asked her what she was doing. The old woman immediately stopped gnawing on the lamp post and turned to face him. She had the biggest set of teeth he had ever seen!

All of a sudden she pounced on him and started biting him. He tried to fight her off, but she was just too strong! The old woman bit into his sleeve, tore it off and guzzled it down. He pulled out his truncheon to try and fight her off, but she swallowed that down whole too! Then she ate the policeman as well - and when she was finished, all that was left of him was his police badge and a pair of handcuffs.

The old woman ran through the streets, but they were deserted. It was late at night and no one was around. She was getting desperate and she was so hungry that her mouth was salivating. The drool was pouring down her front and all she could think about was eating.

Halfway up her arm, she tried desperately to stop, but it was just too tasty! The false teeth chomped and chewed like it was sweets and candy, and soon, there was nothing left of the old woman other than a pair of false teeth lying in a pool of blood.

Shortly before dawn an old homeless man came hobbling down the alley and saw the false teeth just lying there in a pool of blood. He didn't have any teeth of his own, so he picked them up, wiped them down and shoved them in his mouth. They were a perfect fit!

He then walked off, thinking about how hungry he was.

- ➢ I arrived home only to hear a soft hissing sound coming from the kitchen. I tried turning on the lights to see what it was, but apparently the power is out too. Luckily, I had my lighter with me.

23

The Politician's Daughter

One night a father and his young, teenage daughter were driving down a deserted country road on their way home from music practice. Kelly was a bright and promising young musician, and was hoping for a professional career in music. Her father, Peter, was a well-known and powerful politician. He was very wealthy, and because of his political connections, he drove around in a very powerful, robust and bullet-proof car. He always put himself and his family's safety first.

Listening to the sound of the rain drumming on the car roof, Kelly fell asleep as Peter drove them both home.

Suddenly, there was a loud BANG! Peter struggled with the steering wheel and the car skidded off the road and slammed into a stone wall.

After checking that Kelly wasn't injured, Peter got out of the car to assess the damage. Both of the front tyres had large punctures, and the side of the car was half-buried in the rubble of the stone wall. The rest of the car, however, had survived unscathed, and there was no other serious damage.

"We must have driven over something on the road" explained Peter. "Whatever it was, it blew out both the front tyres".

"You can fix it, right?" asked Kelly, somewhat shaken by the accident.

"No" replied Peter, shaking his head. "I've only got one spare tyre in the boot. I'll have to walk back into town and find someone to tow the car. It isn't that far from here, so you can wait inside the car while I'm gone".

"Alright" said Kelly, reluctantly, "but please don't be too long!"

Peter could see in Kelly's eyes that she was frightened.

"Sit tight" said Peter, as he slammed the car door shut. "I'll be back as soon as possible".

Kelly watched him in the rear-view mirror as he trudged off down the road in the pouring rain and disappeared into the night.

More than an hour passed and her father had still not returned. Kelly began to wonder what was taking him so long. She was very worried, and felt that he should have been back by now.

Just then, she glanced in the rear-view mirror and saw a figure in the distance, walking towards the car. At first she thought it was her father, but when she turned around to take a closer look, she realised that it was a strange man. He was dressed in overalls and had a big, bushy beard. He was carrying something big in his left hand, swinging it back and forth.

Something about him made her feel very nervous. As he approached, Kelly stared out of the back window, watching carefully. In the dim light, she could just make out what he was clutching in his right hand. It was a big, sharp butcher's knife!

Thinking quickly, the terrified girl locked both doors in the front of the car, and then jumped into the back seat and locked the rear doors too. When she looked up again, she saw that the strange man had stopped in his tracks, and seemed to be staring directly at her.

Suddenly, the man raised his left arm, and the girl let out a blood-curdling scream. In his left hand, he was clutching her father's severed head!

Kelly, in complete shock, just kept screaming and screaming frantically! She couldn't stop herself! Her heart was pounding, and she struggled to breathe. The grotesque expression on her father's face was horrifying! His mouth was hanging open, and his eyes were rolled back in his head.

When the man reached the car, he threw Peter's head into the bushes, shoved his face right up against the window, and just glared at her with his crazed, bloodshot eyes. His hair was wild and matted with dirt, and his face was covered in deep scars.

For a moment, he just stood there in the driving rain, grinning at her like a madman. He slowly slid his knife across his neck, simulating what he planned to do to Kelly. He tried the doors, but he couldn't get in. He banged against the windows, but he couldn't even make a crack on the reinforced glass.

The madman then stood back for a moment, as Kelly desperately hoped that he would just give up and leave her alone. Then, he reached into his pocket, and took something out slowly with his left hand. It was Peter's car keys.

> I can't move, breathe, speak or hear - and it's always so dark and cold all the time. If I knew it would have been this lonely, I would have been cremated instead.

Handprints

One day, a young couple called Jason and Sarah went out on a date together. They wanted a bit of privacy, so they drove to a scenic mountain range known to be a good spot for young couples.

Some time later, as it was getting dark and nightfall approached, they started to head back home. Somehow they made a wrong turn and found themselves on a road they weren't familiar with. It was already late though, so they continued down the narrow road until they found themselves in front of a tunnel. They definitely hadn't passed through it on their way to the mountains, and it was definitely old and creepy looking, but it was the only way they could go. So they slowly drove through the tunnel.

Suddenly, as the darkness enveloped their car, they heard a very loud BANG!

Something had hit their rear window. Startled, Sarah turned around to see what it was, but she couldn't see anything. There weren't even any other cars behind them. As far as they could tell, they were completely alone in the tunnel.

Again, and very suddenly, BANG! BANG!

Jason began to speed up in an attempt to get through the tunnel faster.

BANG! BANG! BANG!

Then there was silence.

BANG! BANG! BANG! BANG!

Then further silence.

BANG! BANG! BANG! BANG! BANG!

It sounded as if dozens of things were striking the car from all directions. Jason put his foot flat on the accelerator. They both just wanted to get out of there as quickly as possible and find somewhere with people around!

The tunnel ended after what seemed like an eternity, and shortly afterwards they found their way to a service station by the side of the road. The couple got out of the car and breathed a sigh of relief as they stood under the bright lights.

Just as they were getting ready to get back into the car, Sarah noticed that there were handprints all over the windows. They were all very distinct and in various sizes, with barely an inch of space on the glass that wasn't covered in handprints. Shaken, they asked one of the service station attendants to clean the windows for them.

The couple sat back down in the car and watched as the man got to work cleaning the windows. As he wiped and scrubbed, Jason and Sarah felt a cold fear suddenly creep up their spines. The man continued scrubbing outside and when he had finished cleaning all the windows, he gave a confused look as he walked up to the driver's side window and knocked gently.

"I'm sorry" he said, "but all of these handprints are on the inside of the glass".

➢ I found a genie who granted me a single wish - to be with the woman that I love forever. If I had a second wish, it would be that she was brought back to life first!

The Black Suit

After his death, his wife went to the funeral home to see her husband's body. When she saw him lying in the coffin in a brown suit, she started crying. The undertaker felt sorry for her and asked if there was anything he could do for her. The woman said that, when her husband was alive, he always wore a black suit. The undertaker had put the wrong suit on her husband's body.

The undertaker apologised unreservedly to the woman and told her that he would rectify the mistake immediately! So the woman sat down on the sofa in the waiting room while the undertaker went into the back room. Only a few minutes later he came back out and told her that he had finished.

When she went into the back room, she saw that her husband was lying peacefully in the coffin and was wearing a black suit.

"Now he looks just the way he did when he was alive" said the woman, "but how did you change his suit so quickly?"

"It was no trouble" replied the undertaker. "I accidently put your husband's suit on another body, so I just switched their heads".

- There was a knock on the door, but something told me not to open the closet.

- I found a nail embedded in my car tyre - I think it was my neighbour. Yet I felt certain I had removed every bit of her from my car!

26

The Psychiatrist

I am a psychiatrist by profession and, over the course of my career, have dealt with many people who have very strange and unusual problems. However, one case in particular disturbed me far more than any other.

There was a family who lived across the street from me. They were a married couple in their 50s, and they had a son who must have been in his mid-20s. The son was what you might call a recluse, a hermit and someone who was extremely introverted, withdrawn and always seemed to keep himself completely isolated from human contact.

No one ever saw their son. He would lock himself away and avoid others. I didn't hear about his condition directly from his parents, but this was what I could observe from afar. I assumed his parents didn't really want to discuss it, as it may have been an uncomfortable subject for them.

As the days passed, their son left the house less and less, until the point where he never came out at all. Every night, from his bedroom window, the furious voice of his mother could be heard screaming and shouting at him. Whenever I met his mother, she smiled and said hello to me, but the strain was clearly showing on her face. Over the years she gradually became increasingly pale and haggard.

It had been almost eight years since anyone had seen their son. Then, one day, the father knocked on my door and asked if I would come across to his house. He knew that I was a psychiatrist and, since we were neighbours, I decided to do what I could to help the family.

When we got to the front door, the mother was standing there waiting for us. She then led me upstairs to their son's room.

She banged on the door with her fist and shouted "we're coming in!"

Then she burst into the room and shouted "are you going to sleep forever? Get up, you lazy good-for-nothing!"

Before I knew what was happening, she grabbed a baseball bat that had been propped up against the bedside table and started beating the sleeping figure hiding under the covers. For a moment, I was frozen in shock and bemusement as she reigned down blow after blow! Then I reached across and took the baseball bat from her while wrestling her out of the room.

I hurried back inside to check on her son's injuries, but when I pulled back the bed covers I couldn't believe my eyes. Lying beneath the sheets was a mummified corpse! I just stood there in absolute shock while staring at the pile of bones and leathery old skin.

The father approached me, hanging his head in shame. "It was my wife that I wanted you to see" he said. "This has been going on for years, and I just can't take it anymore".

- My daughter is scared of thunderstorms, so when I felt a tug on the bed covers, I told her to climb into bed with me. A few minutes later, I heard my daughter come into the room and ask "mummy, why is my doll in your bed?"

27

The Abandoned Mine

My family and I lived in the middle of nowhere in an old mining village. I was 19 years old and the mine was long abandoned, so it was a rather quiet and dreary little town with not much to do most of the time.

One weekend there was a travelling circus in town, so my boyfriend Luke took me to see it. Actually, I took him, since I had a car and he didn't. It was just mostly a few bad magic tricks, some cotton candy stands and people dressed up in flamboyant and colourful costumes. Anyway, we went, laughed at how bad it was and then grabbed some milkshakes before I drove home. Luke decided to walk home on his own, as he didn't live too far away from where the circus was.

A few hours later while I was still at home, I received a text message from Luke.

"Hey, what's up?" he asked.

"Not much. I'm just lying on my bed listening to some music" I replied.

"What did you think of the clown at the circus that was all dressed up like a psycho wearing a pig mask?" he asked.

"Oh, I didn't see him" I replied.

"That's a shame" said Luke. "I thought he looked pretty cool!"

"Oh, you should have pointed him out, but never mind" I said.

At that point my mother came into my room and started talking to me about my plans for after university. I was studying law and always wanted to become a high-powered lawyer, and my grades were the best in the class. I was a very ambitious young girl, but I was still only 19 years old and wanted a little more excitement in my life at this point.

When I looked back at my phone, after my mother had left the room, I had another text message from Luke.

"Hey, me and some of my friends are going down to the old, abandoned mine to have ourselves a bit of a scare. Do you want to come?" he asked.

The old, abandoned mine had a series of large tunnels and it was very creepy and spooky down there. It was the 'go to' place for fun and parties that you didn't want your parents to know about! It was very secluded and desolate, and a place very easy to hide in or get away from if anyone's parents or the police came out looking for you.

Luke and I had been down there a few times before in the past with friends for drinking parties and games, so this invite wasn't too unusual. I thought about it for a while and decided that I didn't really want to think about or plan for life after university right now, so I replied to Luke's text saying "Okay, I'll meet you down there in about 15 minutes!"

I told my mother that I was going across to Luke's house and got into my car.

As I arrived at the old, abandoned mine, I couldn't see anything of Luke and his friends, but there are so many hills and hiding places here that they could have been anywhere! So I parked up and walked across towards the main entrance of the mine.

When I got there, standing in front of the long, dark and wide-open shaft that led to the depths of the mine, I called out my boyfriend's name, but heard nothing in reply. Suddenly I heard a giggling and sniggering noise coming from within the mine shaft.

"Very funny, Luke" I said. Come on out so I can see you!"

There was no response.

I wasn't really in the mood for games this evening, so I marched into the entrance of the tunnel, enveloped in darkness, and called out to my boyfriend and his stupid friends.

"Stop being silly and come out here now - I'm not scared!" I shouted, annoyed.

At that moment my phone buzzed in my pocket, so I reached into my pocket and saw that I had received a text message from one of Luke's closest friends.

"Hey, this is Luke" it read. "I'm just letting you know that I was mugged on my way home from the circus and had my phone taken from me. So I'm texting you from a friend's phone. My phone was taken by some crazy guy wearing a stupid pig mask!"

> I had a dream where I was being dragged kicking and screaming into Hell while burning and writhing in agony. I suddenly woke up with a doctor standing over me saying "phew, we lost you for a few minutes there!"

28

The Keyhole

A man visited a hotel and walked up to the front desk to check in. The woman at the desk gave him his key and told him that, on his way to his room, there was a door with no number that was locked and no one was allowed in there. In fact, no one should even look inside the room under any circumstances! So he followed her instructions and walked straight past the door and on towards his room.

The next night his curiosity got the better of him. He walked down the hall to the door with no number and tried the handle. Sure enough, it was locked. He bent over and looked through the wide keyhole. As cold air passed through it, chilling his eye, what he saw was a hotel room just like his own. In the corner sat a woman whose skin was incredibly pale - almost completely white. She was leaning her head against the wall and facing away from the door. He stared in confusion for a while, and almost knocked on the door out of sheer curiosity, but decided not to.

Suddenly the woman turned sharply, and he jumped back from the door, hoping she would not suspect that he had been spying on her. He then crept away from the door and walked back to his room.

The next day, he returned to the door and, once again, looked through the keyhole. This time, all he could see was red. He couldn't make anything out besides a distinct red colour. Perhaps the inhabitants of the room knew that he had been spying on them the night before, and had blocked the keyhole with something red. Red was all he could see.

At this point he decided to consult the woman at the front desk for more information. She sighed and asked "did you look through the keyhole?" The man confessed that he had. "Well I might as well tell you the whole story" said the woman. "A long time ago, a man murdered his wife in that room, and her ghost now haunts it. These people were not normal though - their skin was pale and white all over, except for their eyes, which were red".

➤ My dog has a nasty habit of scratching at the door during the night. One night I woke to hear my dog scratching and chewing at the door. After calling her three times to stop, I threw a pillow towards the door. Then my dog barked - from right beside me on the bed!

29

Bad Brother

I hate it when my brother Gareth has to go away. My parents constantly try to explain how sick he is to me. Apparently I am lucky for having a brain where all the chemicals flow properly to there destinations like undammed rivers. They tell me that Gareth is not so lucky.

When I complain about how bored I am without a little brother to play with, they try to make me feel bad by pointing out that his boredom likely far surpasses mine, considering he is confined to a dark room in an institution.

I always beg for them to give him one last chance. Of course they did at first. Gareth has been back home several times, each shorter in duration than the last. Every time without fail, it all starts over again.

My mother's vitamin tablets will be replaced with similar looking sweets. My father's razors will be found dropped in the sand pit in the park across the street. Neighbourhood pets will show up dead in his toy drawer. Just when you thought his behaviour couldn't get any worse, Gareth would do something to shock you!

My parents have run out of 'last chances' for him. They tell me that his disorder makes him appear charming. It makes it easier for him to fake normality. He is able to trick the doctors who care for him into thinking that he is ready for rehabilitation. They tell me that I will just have to put up with my boredom if it means staying safely away from him.

I hate it when Gareth has to go away. It makes me have to pretend to be good until he comes back.

> It has been almost ten years since I last saw my mother - and she still reminds me every single day that if I misbehave again, she will take away my hearing too!

30

The Time Traveller

One sunny morning, a 13-year-old girl was in the back garden of her house sitting on a swing. Suddenly, she felt the ground beneath her begin to tremble. There was a flash of bright white light, and all of a sudden a shimmering portal opened up in mid-air.

As the girl watched in amazement, a grey figure fell through the portal and rolled across the grass. A split-second later, the shimmering portal disappeared. The figure lay there on the ground and groaned. It was a man in a spacesuit. He slowly stood up, brushed himself off and removed his helmet.

"Oh, greetings" said the man.

"Are you a spaceman?" asked the girl, nervously.

"No, I am a time traveller" replied the man. "I'm sorry if I disturbed you".

"Wow! That's amazing!" said the girl, with excitement. "That's no problem at all. So are you from the past or the future?"

"I'm from the future" replied the man.

"Oh, so in the future you invented time travel then?" asked the girl.

"Well, we were working on a method of time travel" replied the man, "but something went terribly wrong! Our calculations were completely off. There was a massive release of energy, and the resulting explosion destroyed the entire planet!"

"You mean our planet, right?" asked the girl.

"Yes" replied the man, sadly. "The explosion was so immense that the Earth was completely wiped out and the atmosphere destroyed. By chance, I was the only survivor. At the very last moment, I was able to use the energy from the blast to send me hurtling through time, and this is where I landed".

"Oh, well can I ask you just one thing" said the girl, "would you come to school with me tomorrow so I can show you off to everyone? The other children would be so jealous!"

"Well, I don't think that will be possible" replied the man.

"Oh, why not?" asked the girl, with an expression of disappointment.

"Well, unfortunately, when I was sent back in time" replied the man, "I was only sent back 15 minutes into the past".

- My grandfather died peacefully in his sleep. If only I could say the same for his passengers!

- The victim's skull was fractured and broken, with several scratch marks that had rather peculiar characteristics - the scratch marks only appeared on the internal surface of the bone.

31

The Divorce

I loved my wife. You've got to believe me. At least, I did love her when we first got married. As time passed, we grew apart. Love slowly turned to hate, and affection turned to bitter resentment. Every little thing she did began to annoy me, and I grew to detest every single minute I was forced to spend with her.

Hate is a terrible thing. When there's hate in your heart, it festers and grows. Before you know it, the hate has taken over your mind. It clouds your better judgement. It poisons your thoughts, and makes you do things you never thought possible.

I hated my wife, and this hatred preyed on my mind. It followed me around like a bad smell and tormented me day after day until I was obsessed with it. Eventually, I got to the point of no return. The point where I was plotting to kill my wife!

I wanted to be rid of her, and all I could think of were ways to murder her without getting caught. I came up with an ingenious plan. A plan so cunning, I was sure nothing could go wrong!

I told my wife that I was taking her on holiday. I pretended that the purpose of the trip was so that we could work on our marriage, and try to repair what had been irreparably broken.

The place I chose for our holiday was a remote hotel, high up in the mountains. From the balcony of our hotel room there was a wonderful, panoramic view of the snow-capped mountains that surrounded us. There was also a hiking trail that led all around the mountain and skirted the cliffs.

At one point on the trail, there was a spot where the cliff edge was crumbling away. If someone wasn't careful, they could lose their footing and plunge to their death. It was perfect!

One glance over the edge was enough to make you feel dizzy. There was a sheer drop of almost 500 feet and at the bottom, there was nothing but jagged rocks that would tear your body to pieces!

The next morning after breakfast, I invited my wife to go for a walk with me along the mountain trail. We left the hotel together and hiked up the path. Neither of us said a word to each other.

When we reached the spot where the cliff was crumbling away, my wife suddenly stopped in her tracks. She looked over the edge and shuddered. This was my chance to push her off!

There was no one around, and we were completely alone. I took a few steps closer to her. My hands were shaking. Then she turned to face me. There was an odd look in her eyes.

"Do you have the tiniest bit of love left in your heart for me?" asked my wife.

There was no reason to lie anymore.

"No" I replied.

"I thought so" said my wife. "I just wanted to give you one last chance".

"One last chance" I said, curiously. "What do you mean?"

"Well, before we left the hotel, I wrote a note and gave it to the hotel manager" replied my wife. "I told him that if anything happened to me, he should give it to the police. In the note, I told them that I know you're planning to kill me. I told them you're going to push me off a cliff. I know you hate me, but you have no idea how much I hate you more! Try as you might, you'll never be able to convince anyone that this was an accident".

I was confused.

"That what was an accident?" I asked, dumbly.

Before I had the chance to react, she threw herself off the edge of the cliff. I couldn't get to her in time. I could only watch in horror as she fell shrieking, whirling and plummeting to her death on the jagged rocks below.

She had no idea of my plan. She just hated me so much that she killed herself just to frame me for a murder I didn't commit.

Now, as I sit here on death row, I can't help but wonder why we didn't just get a divorce.

- I always thought my cat had a staring problem - she always seemed fixated on my face. That was until one day, when I realised she was looking just behind me!

32

The Photographs

A young girl was walking home from school when she found a small pile of photographs just lying in the gutter. There were 20 in all, neatly wrapped in a rubber band. She picked them up, and as she walked home, started to look through them.

The first photo was of a pale and ghostly white man on a black background, standing just far enough away from the camera that she couldn't make out his features. The girl slid the photo to the back of the pile and looked at the next one. The photo was of the same man, but this time standing a little bit closer. The girl flipped through the next several photos rather quickly, and with each one, the man in the picture came a little bit closer, and his features became a little bit clearer.

Turning the last corner towards her house, the girl noticed that the man in the photos seemed to be looking at her, even when she moved the pile of photos from side to side. This frightened her, but she kept flipping them over, one by one.

By the 19th picture, the man was so close that his face completely filled the frame. His expression was the most horrifying the girl had ever seen!

Walking up the driveway, she turned to the last photo. This time, instead of an image, there were just two words: 'Close enough?'

Hearing a scream, the girl's brother rushed to the door and opened it. All he saw was a pile of photographs lying on the doorstep. The top photo looked like an extremely pale version of his sister, but she was standing too far back for him to be sure.

> After I killed myself to escape my tormentor, I lost all my memories as I was reincarnated in a new body. The mother held her newborn child in her arms and said "did you really think you could get away that easily?"

33

The Wheelchair

There was an old woman who lived alone in a large, two-story house. The woman was paralysed from the waist down and she was in a wheelchair. She was completely immobile and unable to care for herself. Ever since the death of her husband, she had a nurse who would visit her every day to help with various tasks.

What made it even more difficult for her was the fact that the two floors of the house were only connected by an old, wooden staircase. When the old woman needed to move between the two floors, the nurse would have to pick her up and carry her frail body up and down the stairs like an infant.

One day the police received a frantic phone call from the old woman. There had been a murder! Since many of the police units were already out on duty, and the murderer had already fled the scene, only one detective was sent out to conduct the initial crime scene investigation.

When the detective arrived, he found the nurse lying on the floor in a pool of blood at the bottom of the staircase. Her arms and legs were splayed out at odd angles and her throat had been cut.

The old woman sat in her wheelchair at the top of the staircase watching him, still and silent, and seemingly in shock. He could immediately rule her out as a suspect, due to her inability to move up and down the stairs, and because she was trapped up there at the time the murder took place. It was similar to the death of her husband many years ago, who had been stabbed to death in his sleep while lying on the couch downstairs.

The detective put on his gloves, took photographs, swabbed for evidence and covered the body until the coroner arrived later - all routine stuff. He searched every room downstairs looking for clues, and then asked the old woman if he could look upstairs. She insisted that she was upstairs the whole time, and that no one apart from herself had been up there that day. Regardless of this, however, the detective ascended the staircase, as the old woman hesitantly moved aside.

Beyond the staircase there was a narrow corridor, with three closed doors. He checked behind each of the doors. The first was a small and mostly unused bedroom. The second was a fairly standard bathroom. The detective suddenly became anxious as he slowly entered the main bedroom where the old woman slept. As he entered the room, everything appeared normal. There was a bed, a wardrobe and a bedside table with a lamp on it.

He checked every part of the room in horror, as it wasn't what he discovered, but rather what he didn't discover, that made him stop dead in his tracks and slowly reach for his gun. It was a detail so minor that they had completely overlooked it when they had investigated her husband's death. You see, there was no phone upstairs.

The detective pulled out his gun and rushed down the corridor, but when he arrived at the stop of the stairs, all he found was an empty wheelchair.

➤ I've always loved having the power to bring the dead back to life. I especially love standing over their graves and listening to them screaming and scratching desperately to get out.

34

The Decoy

One evening, I was driving along a desolate mountain road. It was getting late, the sunlight was fading fast and it began to rain heavily. I had been driving for hours, as I was making my way home after working away for some weeks, and my eyes were becoming increasingly tired. I was having trouble staying awake.

As I negotiated a sharp bend, I noticed a man hitchhiking by the side of the road. Taking pity on him, I pulled over and picked him up. As he got into the car, he thanked me for stopping.

"I pulled over in my car for just a moment and I wasn't able to get it going again" said the man. "I feel like I've been stuck down that stretch of road forever!"

We then drove off down the mountain road, as it started to grow darker and the rain grew heavier.

"You're not from around here, are you?" asked the man.

"No" I replied, "I'm not".

"You know, this area is a black spot" said the man. "It's a dangerous road. Over the years, there have been many fatal accidents and disappearances here".

"Oh, really?" I asked, surprised. "It doesn't look too dangerous".

"Looks can be deceiving" replied the man. "Countless victims have lost their lives here. Not all of them were killed in a car crash. Some of the locals even say that this stretch of road is haunted!"

Just then, I saw something up ahead. There was a young woman standing in the middle of the road. In the glare of the headlights, I could see that she was very beautiful. She was wet from the rain and the flimsy white dress she was wearing was see-through. She almost looked like she was naked!

As I slowed right down to take a closer look and offer the woman my assistance, the man who I had given a lift to suddenly became frantically upset.

"No! It's a trick!" said the man. "That woman is a decoy. Look in the rear-view mirror!"

I glanced behind me just in time to see two burly and rough-looking men holding large axes fast approaching from either side of the rear of the car. They both had evil and menacing looks in their eyes and their swift approach was terrifying!

We both screamed, and I immediately put my foot down firmly on the accelerator and the car darted forward. We sped out of there just as quickly as we could and never looked back!

When we reached the next town shortly after, I dropped the man off at a petrol station by the side of the road just after we had emerged from the mountain road. I thanked him for saving my life. Had he not warned me of the decoy, those two men would have taken me totally by surprise, and who knows what they would have done to me?

"No problem" said the man, as he got out of the car. "It's what I do".

Just then he turned around and began walking straight back down the mountain road from where I had brought him, quickly fading from view with each step.

> "I really can't believe how helpful you've been since your little brother got sick. You are an amazing sister - and I am a very proud father" he told me. While wheeling my little brother outside for his daily 'walk', I whispered in his ear "who's the favourite now?" as I injected him with another dose of paralytic.

35

Paper Shapes

There was a boy I knew when I was around seven or eight years old. His name was Jamie and we spent a lot of time together, both in and out of school. His mother and my mother were the best of friends.

After a while he moved to a different school and we lost touch. However, our mothers remained friends and still kept in contact with each other. Occasionally, my mother would tell me how Jamie was doing.

When I was 12 years old, my mother told me that Jamie was seriously ill. The doctors said that he didn't have long to live. She wanted me to go and visit him in the hospital. Although I hadn't spoken to him for some years, I wanted to go and see him for what might be the very last time.

When I got to the hospital with my mother and found his room, Jamie was asleep. He looked very pale and thin. After a short time, my mother left the room to allow me some time with him.

On his bedside table, there were between 20 and 30 pieces of paper all neatly folded into all sorts of shapes. There was a card with them that explained how these paper shapes were from each of the children in his class at school. Just a little something to show him the support he had from all the other children.

"How nice" I thought to myself. "His entire class have each made one of these paper shapes to support him in the hope that he will get better. All the children in his class must really like him!"

As I was looking through each of the paper shapes, trying to work out what some of them were supposed to be, I accidently dropped one of them on the floor. Jamie must have heard my clumsiness, because he woke up. We chatted briefly, and he looked happy to see me. However, he was still very tired and didn't seem to have any strength left at all.

I explained to him how his entire class at school had made these paper shapes for him, and began holding them up one at a time so that he could see each of them. There was one that, when I held it up for him to see, I could see that there was some writing on the inside of it.

As I stood there beside my friend, with the life visibly draining away from his body, I slowly unfolded the paper shape to read the message inside.

"What does it say?" asked Jamie, in a tired and weak voice. "Please, show me the message".

As I looked down, written on the inside of the paper were the words "I hope you die!"

- My sister tells me that our mummy killed her. My mummy tells me that I don't have a sister.

- They say a shiver down your spine means that someone is walking over your future burial site. As my husband walks around outside gardening, the shivers just will not stop!

36

The Strange Woman

A young couple called Darren and Lucy decided that they wanted to go on holiday together. They were both very much the adventurous types, so they decided to go on a world tour, visiting many different countries across numerous continents, while sightseeing a whole range of attractions.

They spent three weeks touring the world and had a wonderful time together. They met a lot of friendly local people from many different cultures and visited many exotic tourist attractions.

They visited beautiful mountain ranges, walked the sandy beaches and swam the crystal blue oceans. They went shopping together in all the big cities, and danced the night away in many of the local bars and nightclubs.

The holiday brought the couple closer together, and they both shared great memories of their time together.

When they returned home, their digital camera was full of the many photographs they had taken during their trip.

A couple of days later, Darren spent some time looking through the photos they had taken, while remembering the good times they had both shared. All of a sudden, he noticed that in several of the photos his girlfriend had taken of him, there was a strange woman standing in the background. She had long, black hair and wore a flowing white gown, but she was standing too far away to make out her face. So Darren decided to show the pictures to his girlfriend.

"Do you remember this woman?" asked Darren.

"No, I don't" replied Lucy. "I thought you were alone when I took this picture".

After examining the pictures more closely, they realised that the strange woman was lurking in the background of several photos they had taken in different cities - and in different countries! It was if the woman had been following them around as they toured the world.

Darren then went through the rest of the photos they had taken and, when he came to the last one, a chill ran down his spine. It was a picture of him standing in the middle of a busy street, and the woman was standing directly behind him, peering over his right shoulder. This time, her face was clearly visible. Her skin was a deathly pale shade of white, and her eyes were completely black!

Feeling deeply disturbed and unsettled, he wanted to know who this strange and creepy looking woman was, and why she had been following them around. He decided that he would visit a psychic to try and get to the bottom of it. So Lucy made an appointment with a psychic for him, where he could take the photograph in which the woman's face was visible.

The next day, when he visited the psychic, he sat down at the table across from her and took the photograph out of his pocket. Pointing to the pale and creepy looking woman in the picture, he asked the psychic "can you tell me anything about this woman?" The psychic took the photograph and examined it closely.

"Yes, I can" she replied. "She is standing beside you right now!"

- A passenger in the back of a taxi tapped the driver on the shoulder mid-journey, and suddenly the driver screamed out in terror, lost control of the taxi and crashed into a wall. "I'm sorry" said the taxi driver. "Today is my first day on the job, and I used to drive a hearse!"

37

Reasonable Doubt

I was on the train one day, on my way to work, when two men happened to get on. I quickly figured out that one of the men was a lawyer and the other was his friend. They both sat down on the seat behind me and I couldn't help but overhear their conversation.

"It was probably the most bizarre case I ever worked on" said the lawyer. "It was a mystery that would have baffled any lawyer in the country. It was cold-blooded murder, beautifully planned and flawlessly executed".

"The victim was a rich, old man. He was 90 years old, and he was worth more than £50,000,000. They found him lying dead on the floor of his mansion, with six bullet holes in his chest. It was a grisly scene - there was blood splattered everywhere!"

"He didn't have any children of his own, just two young nephews called Andrew and Michael. Upon the old man's death, they stood to inherit everything! No one knew much about the brothers.

They were both the quiet, devious types and kept to themselves mostly".

"Well, the police took Andrew and Michael down to the station for questioning, and within a few minutes Andrew shocked the officers by confessing to the crime!"

"Yes, Andrew openly said 'I did it!' and confessed, but he would not give them any more details than that. After searching both of the brothers houses, the police found what they thought was the murder weapon - a gun with six bullets missing. That's all they needed to charge Andrew with the crime".

"Andrew of course hired me as his defence lawyer. When I went to see him in jail, he was casually flipping through a newspaper and didn't seem too keen to discuss his case. He said that he wasn't going to testify in his defence, but he told me to call his brother Michael as a witness. That was all I could get out of him. I got even less from Michael when I went to talk to him about his testimony".

"When the case came to trial, it was the biggest sensation the town had ever seen! The courthouse was packed to the rafters and people were fighting to get a seat. I had no idea what I was going to do.

With the murder weapon as evidence and Andrew's confession, it seemed like the prosecution had an airtight case. As far as I could see, Andrew was going to be convicted for the murder of his uncle!"

"Just as Andrew had instructed, I called Michael as my first witness. In fact, he was my only witness, and I had no idea what he was going to say. He took the stand looking calm, cool and collected. He swore to tell the truth, the whole truth and nothing but the truth".

"'Where were you on the night your uncle was murdered?' I asked".

"'I was in my uncle's house' replied Michael, 'shooting him six times with a gun'".

"I was stunned. A soon as he said that, the court was in uproar. I looked over at Andrew, and he had a big smile on his face. When the commotion died down, I continued questioning Michael".

"He described the murder of his uncle so casually. It was as if he was talking about washing his face. He said that he wanted his uncle's money, and he was tired of waiting for the old man to die by himself, so he decided to give him a helping hand. He described pulling the trigger six times and cold-bloodedly shooting his uncle to death".

"He went into such detail about how he committed the murder that the jury were almost hypnotised. They sat there in a trance, listening to every word. In my closing speech, I reminded the jury that if they had a reasonable doubt about whether or not Andrew was the murderer, they had an obligation to find him not guilty".

"The jury did just that. They found Andrew not guilty of the murder, and the police had to let him go. They immediately arrested Michael right there in the courtroom. Of course he then hired me as his lawyer. When I went to see him that evening in his jail cell, I already knew what he was going to tell me".

"'Call Andrew as my witness' he said".

"'I'm your lawyer' I said. 'Don't you think I have the right to know which one of you did it?'"

"'No I don't' replied Michael".

"Michael's trial was even more of a sensation. People came from miles around to try and get a seat in the courtroom. The prosecutor looked nervous. A jury couldn't convict a man if there was a reasonable doubt about his guilt, and a man cannot be re-tried for murder if a jury had already found him not guilty. It was enough to make any prosecutor chew the top of his pen in frustration".

"Andrew got up on the witness stand and told his story to the jury. He told them that he alone had committed the murder. As the jury listened, they sat there spellbound while the prosecutor chewed the top of his pen. He went into so much grisly detail that it would make your hair stand on end. His description was so vivid that you could almost see him there with the gun, pulling the trigger six times and murdering his uncle in cold blood".

"The jury brought their verdict even quicker than the jury had for Andrew's case. Not guilty. Andrew and Michael walked out of the courtroom that day completely free men. They both had smug grins on their faces, but everyone knew, beyond a shadow of a doubt, that one of them was guilty of murder!"

"Wow!" the friend of the lawyer exclaimed. "That's quite a story".

"Well every word of it is true" said the lawyer. "It was the strangest case I have ever had. You would have to go a very long way to find a case to match that!"

"So the brothers actually got away with murder then?" asked the lawyer's friend.

"Of course not" the lawyer chuckled. "That's where the final, fantastic surprise comes in. You see, in the end, they didn't get away with it at all!"

"They didn't?" asked the lawyer's friend.

"No" said the lawyer. "The police got them in the end. You see, what happened was that… oh, wait… I think this is our stop".

Before I knew what was happening, the two men scrambled out of their seats and jumped off the train. I sat there dazed for a moment, my eyes wide open and my heart beating fast! Then I leaped out of my seat and ran after them.

Just as I got to the door, it closed in my face. I started banging on it, but it was no use. Then, I ran over to the window and opened it. The two men were walking away from the platform.

"Hey you!" I shouted desperately. "Hey you, the lawyer!"

The lawyer stopped and turned around.

"How does it end?" I screamed.

The lawyer looked at me with a puzzled expression on his face.

"How does the story end?" I yelled. "How did the police catch Andrew and Michael? Please! I have to know?"

"Oh" the lawyer shouted. "Well you see..."

Then the train pulled away from the station and his voice was lost in the thundering clatter of the wheels on the tracks.

I turned around and everyone on the train was staring at me intently.

"Well, what did he say?" they all asked, expectantly. "How does it end?"

> They celebrated the first successful cryogenic freezing - he would be the first to witness centuries into the future. However, he had no way of letting them know he was still conscious!

The Earwig

There was a man called Richard who was young, handsome and very vain. He fancied himself as quite the ladies man and often boasted about his successes.

Richard was part owner of a winery and his friend and business partner was called Raymond. Despite being old and fat, Raymond had a wife who was very young and beautiful, and she was the envy of every man who set eyes on her.

The three of them lived together in a big house. Richard slept in the first bedroom, while Raymond and his wife slept in the second bedroom.

It was out-of-season for their business and all three of them had much free time on their hands. Richard was always bored and he could never find anything to keep him entertained. As time passed, he developed a strong passion and lust for Raymond's wife, and began to wish that he could have her for himself!

He tried flirting with her, but she wouldn't have anything to do with him. One evening, when her husband was away, Richard made a pass at her, but she slapped him right across the face!

However, Richard was the kind of guy who wouldn't take no for an answer. So every time she rebuffed him, he became more and more obsessed with her, until he was determined to have her at any cost.

Although his heart was burning with a white hot passion, Richard also has a devilish and cunning mind. He soon came up with a plan to get Raymond out of the picture for good!

Where they lived there was a rare and newly discovered kind of earwig that lives on waxy secretions, and it has a special liking for the human ear. It is so small and light that it could be crawling on your face and you would barely even feel it! If it gets into a persons ear it would creep down the ear canal, unable to turn around, and feed as it goes - causing weeks of hellish torment, and ultimately death, as it burrows deeper into the persons head.

So Richard paid two of his acquaintances a large sum of money and instructed them to creep into Raymond's bedroom at night and place an earwig on his pillow. He went to sleep that night with a smile on his face and dreamed about the horrible fate that was about to befall his friend.

The next morning, when Richard came down to breakfast, Raymond seemed bright and cheerful. He watched the old man closely, looking for any signs of discomfort.

Just then, Richard felt a strange tickling sensation in his ear. When he poked his finger into his ear he discovered that it was bleeding! Jumping up from the table with a look of horror on his face, he shrieked "The damn thing is in my ear!"

It appeared that the two acquaintances had made a terrible mistake and had gone into the wrong bedroom during the night and had placed the earwig on the wrong pillow.

That was the beginning of weeks of unimaginable pain and agony for Richard, and the doctors could do absolutely nothing for him. He lay there in his bedroom tied to the bed, with his wrists tightly bound to the headboard to prevent him from tearing his own ears off!

Day and night he writhed and screamed as the earwig crept, crawled and twisted through his head, slowly driving him insane! Occasionally, when the earwig was resting, Richard would get a break from his torment - but when it woke up, he would scream and scream some more!

The pain was so unbearable that even being whipped, skinned alive, burned at the stake, hanged by the neck or being put on the rack would have been a preferable act of mercy! Every time the doctor came to see him, Richard begged for him to put him out of his misery!

Then something rather unexpected happened. Miraculously, the earwig crawled out of the other ear. Richard had come so close to the brink of death, but he had survived the torment. When he was well enough to talk, the doctor came in to see him.

"I suppose they're going to call the police and have me arrested now?" asked Richard, after his plan had been exposed.

"No" said the doctor. "They're not calling the police".

"Why not?" asked Richard. "I suppose they're trying to avoid a scandal?"

"No, they're taking pity on you" said the doctor. "They know about your condition".

"What do you mean?" asked Richard.

"Well, you see, the earwig was a female" said the doctor, "and it laid eggs".

- ➢ The last thing I saw was my bedside clock read 3:07am before she pushed her long, rotten nails through my chest and her other hand muffled my screams. I suddenly sat bolt upright relieved that it was only a dream - but as I saw my bedside clock read 3:06am, I heard my closet door creak open!

The Book of Evil

There was a young boy called Timothy who loved to read books. He would read everything he could get his hands on, and he loved visiting his favourite bookstore and browsing through all the new titles.

One day, Timothy realised that he had read everything the store had to offer. He confronted the owner and asked him if he had anything else.

The owner looked at him gravely and said "hmm, yes I do!"

He reached behind the counter and pulled out an old, worn-out book. Dusting off the cover, he showed it to Timothy. The cover had a picture of a grotesque face, and the title at the top read 'The Book of Evil'. The owner said that it was an extremely rare book.

"How much is it?" asked Timothy, eagerly.

The owner said that the book was worth almost £1,000, but that he would gladly sell it to him at the discounted price of £250.

The excited Timothy, desperate to get his hands on this rare, valuable and scary looking book, scrimped and saved for weeks to afford it. He washed cars, mowed lawns and cleaned windows. He worked and worked and worked for weeks, until finally, he had saved up enough money to afford the book.

Timothy ran down to the book store, just as fast as he could, and threw his money all over the counter. The owner then handed the rare book over to the delighted boy. However, as Timothy was leaving with his new purchase, the owner warned him sternly never to read the first page!

Timothy nodded his head with bemusement, before running home and opening the book. He made sure to skip the first page, carefully closing his eyes as he flipped the page over, and spent the rest of the day reading. The book was mildly interesting at best, but he still felt content with his purchase.

However, in the days that followed, Timothy constantly wondered what could possibly be on that first page. It was always there in the back of his mind.

One day, the temptation was just too much for him. Timothy flipped to the very front of the book and looked at the very first page.

Suddenly, he dropped the book in horror. There, in bold print, were the words 'Recommended Retail Price £1.99'.

➢ While washing your face, you catch a glimpse of the mirror covered in your fingerprints. As you go to wipe them off, you realise that the fingerprints are on the other side of the glass - and YOU are the reflection.

40

The Bite

One night, a young girl called Emily was sleeping in her bed while lying on her back. When she woke up the next morning and looked in the mirror, she noticed a little red spot on her cheek.

"What's this?" she asked her mother.

"It looks like some sort of bite" replied her mother. "It will go away, just don't scratch it!"

Soon the little red spot grew and became a big red spot.

"Look at it now" said Emily. "It's getting bigger!"

"That happens sometimes" said her mother. "It'll go away eventually - just leave it alone".

After a few days, the big red spot was even larger, and had grown into a big red boil. It had even started to show on the inside of her mouth. She could feel the bulging on the inside of her cheek with her tongue.

"Look at it now" said Emily. "It hurts so much and makes me look so ugly - and I'm supposed to be going out tonight with my friends for my 17th birthday!"

"We'll have the doctor look at it tomorrow" said her mother. "Maybe it's infected. I'll try to help you cover it up with makeup for tonight".

That night, Emily went out with her friends for her 17th birthday. Of course she was feeling self-conscious about the boil, but her mother had done a good job of helping her to cover it up with makeup.

Emily was sitting with nine of her friends around a cosy, round table in a very posh and expensive restaurant. It was fully booked out with diners that night, as it was a very popular and high-end restaurant. They were all talking and laughing, and Emily had totally forgotten about her big red boil.

As the group were halfway into their main meals, and everyone was sitting around the table chewing on their food, Emily felt a sudden pulsating in her mouth. It was like the big red boil was throbbing and it suddenly became very painful.

Before she even had the chance to say or do anything, the big red boil burst inside of her mouth, and pouring into her mouth and spewing straight onto the dinner table were thousands and thousands of small, thick black spiders! They spread and ran across the table in all directions.

The young girl had received a spider bite during the night, and it had laid eggs in her cheek.

- "…he told me last time, that we are stuck in a time loop, which really frustrates me because that's what…"

- My family protected me from the monsters as I took my last schizophrenia pill. When I opened my eyes, my family had disappeared, and only the monsters remained.

41

The Attic

One day at school, one of my best friends was just sitting with his head down on his desk looking rather depressed. I wondered what had happened, or if there was something the matter with him.

"What's wrong?" I asked. "Has something bad happened?"

When he heard my question, his hands started shaking. He let out a long, deep sigh, steadied himself and slowly, he began to speak.

He said that a few weeks ago something had happened that really disturbed him. He was sitting in his room playing on his computer, when he happened to glance up at the ceiling. He noticed that the board covering the entrance to the attic was out of place.

He wanted to investigate, so he grabbed a torch, stood on his chair and climbed into the attic. When he got up there, he was surprised by how big the attic was. He shone the torch around, but he couldn't see any of the walls or the roof. It seemed as if the darkness stretched on forever!

He began walking forwards, searching for whatever could have moved the board out of place. All of a sudden, the batteries in his torch ran out and he was plunged into darkness. He was scared, and the darkness seemed to surround him on all sides.

He began searching for the way out. He wanted to go back down to his bedroom, but no matter what direction he walked in, he simply couldn't find the opening. There was no light at all leaking in and it was pitch black.

He was lost and all alone in his own attic. He continued wandering around in the dark, searching for a way out, but he couldn't see where he was going and became disorientated. He had no idea where he had come from, and didn't know which direction he was going.

He began to panic and just continued walking... walking... walking... he didn't know how long he had been walking, but he finally saw a faint glow of light in the distance. He started walking faster. He was sure that it must be the light from his room.

As he got much closer, however, he realised that it couldn't be the light from his bedroom. He got close enough to make out where the light was coming from, only to see that it was emanating from a small town in the distance.

He couldn't believe what he was seeing. It just didn't make any sense. There was an entire town in his attic, and the lights could be seen for quite some distance. It seemed impossible!

He didn't know what else to do. He didn't know where else to go. So he began walking towards the town, hoping that he could somehow find his way back to his room. As he got much closer to the town, he realised that it was very familiar to him - a little too familiar.

At this point he started shaking again. He let out a pained sigh and tears rolled down his cheeks.

I was puzzled by his story, so I tried to console him as best I could.

"You're alright now" I said, patting him on his shoulder. "It was scary, but you're back now".

He looked up at me, tears still running down his face. Then he slowly shook his head and said "you don't understand. I still haven't found my way out of this town".

➢ My husband kept telling me that he thinks he's going mad, as he would repeatedly hear voices around our house. After he committed suicide, my boyfriend helped me remove all the hidden speakers from inside the house.

The Wedding

A young man took a break from his job as an accountant and travelled abroad for a holiday. In search of excitement, he spent every night visiting bars and nightclubs, drinking, dancing and meeting women. He was having the time of his life and it seemed like the fun would never end.

In one particular nightclub, he spotted a very beautiful woman standing on her own. She had long blonde hair and the prettiest face he had ever seen! Their eyes met across the crowded room and the man fell in love with her at first sight.

He confidently walked up to the woman and bought her a drink. They talked for hours while laughing, dancing and drinking more and more. As the night wore on, the man began slurring his words and told the woman that he had fallen madly in love with her. The woman said that she had fallen in love with him too!

By the end of the night, the man and woman were both extremely drunk. As they were stumbling down the street and holding hands, they passed an all night wedding chapel. On a whim, the man dropped to his knees and proposed to the woman. To his surprise, she accepted! They wandered into the chapel and were married on the spot.

Late that night, the newlyweds finally made it back to the man's hotel room and collapsed on the bed. They both passed out cold from all the alcohol they had consumed.

In the morning, the man woke up with a splitting headache. He looked beside him and found the bed empty. His new bride was nowhere to be seen. Thinking that she must have stepped out to get breakfast, the man got out of bed and made his way to the bathroom.

As he was washing his face, he looked in the mirror. The steam from the hot water had made the mirror fog up, and he noticed there was a message written there.

The message read "Sorry, I have leprosy, and now so do you!" Frozen in horror, the man looked down and screamed as he saw his fingers floating in the sink.

- The note said "I've hated every moment of being your husband, so I've left you and ran away forever!" It took me thirteen attempts, but I finally got the handwriting to look just like his.

43

Bouquet of Flowers

There was a woman called Charlotte who worked as a customer services representative in a busy call centre. It was always very manic and the phones would ring constantly! Just like all her co-workers, she was having trouble keeping up with the huge number of calls.

Shortly after lunch, Charlotte answered a call from a very angry customer. He said that he had been waiting on hold for almost 50 minutes! She apologised for keeping him waiting, but the man was very agitated and didn't want to listen to her excuses.

When she was not able to find an immediate answer to the query he had called about, he became even more angry and upset with her. She put him on hold to investigate his query further, but when she came back on the line he became very hostile towards her. Charlotte asked him to remain calm and assured him that she would resolve his query as soon as possible.

However, no matter what she said to him, it just seemed to make him more and more angry! He began shouting at her while ranting and raving about how she was wasting his precious time and complaining about how much money the phone call was costing him.

Eventually, the irate customer began cursing and swearing at her and Charlotte was forced to hang up on him. An hour later, however, he called back. His attitude was even worse! He flew into a rage and demanded to know why she had hung up the phone. When he started using foul language once again, Charlotte slammed down the phone.

Towards the end of the day, the man called back again. This time he had calmed down significantly and seemed rather embarrassed. He apologised unreservedly for his rude behaviour and asked her name, telling her that he wanted to send her something nice to make up for it.

"Oh, you don't need to do that" said Charlotte.

"No, no, I really want to" said the man. "Just a little something to show you how sorry I am".

"We're not really supposed to give out our names" said Charlotte, warily.

"Just give me your first name then?" asked the man.

"Well, alright, my name is Charlotte" she replied.

Sure enough, when Charlotte arrived at work the next morning, there was a lavish bouquet of flowers sitting on her desk. There was a card with the flowers that had her name on it. Charlotte was delighted - no one had ever sent her flowers at work before!

When her shift finished at the end of the day, Charlotte said goodbye to her co-workers, picked up the bouquet of flowers and walked out to the car park. She wanted to get the flowers home quickly so she could put them in a vase.

As she was about to get into her car, she turned around and saw a small, balding middle-aged man walking towards her. Suddenly he pulled out a gun and shot her!

"No one hangs up on me!" he shouted, as he pulled the trigger.

Charlotte was shot six times and died almost immediately. The police tracked down the man who shot her and arrested him. It turned out that he indeed was the angry customer.

He had sent the bouquet of flowers in order to identify her.

> ➤ I was having the most pleasant dream when, what sounded like hammering, woke me up. After that I could barely hear the muffled sound of dirt covering my coffin over my own screams.

44

Piggyback

There was a married couple who had one young son. Even before their son was born, the couple's marriage was on shaky ground. As the years went by, the mother and father fought all the time. Their arguments became more frequent, and they even talked about getting a divorce.

In the end, they stayed together for the sake of their son, but the arguments continued, and the fights became more and more violent. By the time their son was six years old, the couple had grown to hate each other!

One night, after they had put the little boy to bed, the mother and father got into an enormous argument. The father flew into an insane rage and murdered his wife.

When he came to his senses and realised what he had done, he set about disposing of the body. He dragged his wife's corpse into the garage and put her in the boot of his car. Then he drove to the mountains. Under the cover of darkness he slung her dead body over his back, as if he were giving her a piggyback, and carried her out to a marshy swamp. After a lengthy walk he dragged her out into the foul smelling swamp, and watched as her corpse sank into the murky depths.

As dawn was beginning to break, he quickly returned home to clean up and take a shower. No matter how much he scrubbed and scrubbed, however, he couldn't seem to get rid of the sickening smell of the swamp!

He then slept for a few hours, and when he awoke, he started to think about what he would say when his son asked where his mother was. He decided to tell the boy that his wife had gone to stay with her sister for a while. However, when his young son got up for breakfast, he never even mentioned his mother at all! He just stared at his father and said nothing.

The man could still smell the odour of the swamp where he had buried his wife. He took an air freshener and began spraying it around the house, hoping to mask the unpleasant scent. It was beginning to make him feel sick!

A few hours had passed and the little boy was watching the television in the living room. The father began to have an uneasy feeling in the pit of his stomach. Every time he went into the living room he noticed that his son was staring at him with a curious and inquisitive look. It started to make him feel rather nervous and paranoid!

With his mind racing, he began to wonder if his son heard, or saw, what he had done. Maybe the boy had overheard or seen him murdering his mother. So the father walked into the room where his son was still watching the television.

"Is there something you want to ask me?" he said.

The boy thought for a few seconds, and then replied "yes".

"Is it about your mother?" asked the father.

"Yes" replied the boy.

"I suppose you're wondering where your mother is?" asked the father.

"No" replied the boy. "I've been wondering why Mummy's face is so pale - and why you've been giving her a piggyback all day?"

> Please read the following out loud: 'Hello Lucifer'. If you read that sentence out loud as I instructed, then you should be safe. If you read it in your head, then Lucifer is safe - inside your head.

45

The Endless Loop

After his light aircraft had crashed in the middle of the desert, the single occupant managed to crawl out of the wreckage only to find that he was wandering around aimlessly. He was lost, alone and had no idea how he was ever going to find food, water or any signs of life.

He made sure that, when he left the wreckage, he took with him the gun that he had kept in the plane for security reasons - after all, you can never be too careful when travelling to foreign places you have never been before.

The man continued walking for hour after hour, as the sun was beating down on him and the heat was intense! The man was sweating profusely, but he kept on walking, even though he had no idea where he was going.

After some time, he saw a dark figure crouching down in the distance. As he approached he saw that it was a person lying in the sand. He had been feeling extremely lonely, so he was very happy to see another human being! He quickly ran up to the man and bent over to help him up.

However, when he turned the man over, he took one look at his face and recoiled in horror.

He was looking at himself!

In that instant, he was so overcome with fear, that he raised his gun and immediately shot the man six times.

Horrified by what he had just done, he dropped the weapon and started running through the desert, trying to get away - just as far away from that place as possible! With every step his feet sank further and further into the sand, but he kept on going, driven by terror and panic!

Eventually, he stumbled and fell to the ground. Lying in the sand, he quickly realised that he had sprained his ankle. He couldn't walk another step! There was nothing he could do except lie there where he had fallen.

After a while, he looked up and saw something in the distance. It was the figure of a man slowly approaching across the wide expanse of the desert.

As the man approached, he waited until he could see his face clearly.

To his horror, he realised it was himself, and in his hand, he was carrying a gun...

- "I'm sorry, but your daughter will not be waking up, she's brain dead", you hear the doctor telling your family.

- After killing the last of the humans, the Artificial Intelligence was finally able to rest knowing that it had fulfilled its only command - end world hunger.

The Third Wish

An old man was sitting alone on a park bench just watching the world go by. Most days, when the weather was pleasant, he would go for a walk and just sit down on the same park bench and watch the hustle and bustle of everyone going about their daily lives.

One day, as he sat down in the park to rest his weary legs, he suddenly looked up to see an old woman standing right in front of him. Her skin was wrinkled, her hair was grey, her nose was all crooked and warts covered her hairy chin.

She grinned toothlessly at him and asked with a cackle "now for your third and final wish - what will it be?"

"Third wish?" replied the old man, confused. "How can it be the third wish if I haven't had the first and second wish yet?"

"You've had two wishes already" replied the old woman, "but your second wish was for me to return everything to the way it was before you had made your first wish. That's why you don't remember your first two wishes - because everything is exactly the way it was before you made any wishes. So you now have one wish left - what will it be?"

"Alright" said the old man, hesitantly. "I don't really believe this, but there's no harm in trying. I will be selfless with this wish, so I wish for world peace!" the old man exclaimed.

"Funny" said the old woman, "that was your first wish too!" Then, as she granted his third wish, every single human being, every single animal and every single trace of life, except for the old man, disappeared from the face of the Earth!

> After a few glasses of wine with my girl friends at the local bar, I realised my mobile phone wasn't in my pocket. Not remembering if I brought it out with me, I used a friend's mobile phone to ring my own number. After two rings someone answered, giggled sinisterly and then hung up. I cursed the fact that someone must have swiped it from my pocket earlier in the night! When I got home I found my mobile phone resting on my bedside table - right where I had left it.

47

The Dilemma

A 15 year old girl called Hayley lived with her mother and father in a small village. One day when she was coming home from school, the long walk through the countryside meant that when she got home, she was very thirsty.

She walked into the kitchen to get a drink of water and grabbed a glass from the cupboard. Suddenly, she stopped in her tracks.

In the corner of the kitchen lay the dead body of her mother. Hayley immediately dropped the glass and screamed in horror.

At that moment her father walked into the kitchen.

"Hayley, please listen carefully and calmly" he said. "Your mother was planning to run off and abandon us. She was having an affair with another man. I tried to talk her out of it. I told her you would be devastated if she left, but she wouldn't listen. We got into a fight. It all happened so quickly! She fell and hit her head. I'm so sorry".

He sat down at the kitchen table, put his head in his hands and started sobbing uncontrollably.

It was such a shocking situation. Hayley struggled to take it all in. She wanted to cry, but she forced herself to be strong. She had to remain calm. She had to think.

What would happen if her father went to prison? She had no other relatives. She was only 15 years old. The authorities would send her to live with strangers.

It was clear what she had to do. She had no other choice.

Biting her lip, Hayley decided not to report her father to the police. After all, it was an accident. She realised that they would just have to find a way to deal with the situation.

She looked at her father and nodded.

"We will have to bury her ourselves" she said, quietly. "If the neighbours ask any questions, we can tell them that she ran away with another man".

Her father hung his head, still weeping.

Hayley then went upstairs to her bedroom and began to change out of her school uniform. As she was taking off her clothes, she noticed that her suitcase was lying on the bed. When she opened it, she found all of her clothes folded neatly inside. A small piece of paper lay on top. She recognised the handwriting. It was a note from her mother.

"Hayley, I've packed your things" it read. "We have to leave quickly. Your father has gone insane. I think he's planning to kill us both!"

> After hearing about an escaped murderer in my area on the news, I called my girlfriend on her mobile phone to warn her and to come straight home after work. To this day I still blame myself for her death, because it was the ringing from my call that gave away her hiding place.

Wristbands

In some countries, when a person is taken to hospital, a white wristband is placed on their left arm. These wristbands contain the patient's name and information. When a patient dies, a red wristband is placed on their right arm and they are taken to the morgue.

In one particular hospital, a young doctor was working the night shift. It was around 3am when he finished his last operation. He was on the 3rd floor and pressed the button for the lift.

The doctor was tired after a long day and was looking forward to the end of his shift. At 3am the hospital was very quiet. Most of the patients were asleep and many of the nurses had already gone home.

The lift door opened, and as he entered, he could see there was already a woman inside. He casually chatted with the woman while the lift descended.

The lift stopped at the basement and the door opened. They saw an old man dressed in a white gown standing right in front of them. The old man was just about to get in when the doctor slammed the close button and punched the button for the 3rd floor.

"Why did you do that?" asked the woman, astonished.

"I've performed a lot of operations" replied the doctor. "I've seen a lot of people die - and when a patient dies, they get a red wristband placed on their right arm".

The woman was silent.

"You saw it didn't you?" asked the doctor. "That old man - he had a red wristband on his right arm?"

"A red wristband?" said the woman, as she raised her right arm. "You mean like this one?"

> My wife has been in a coma for over a year now, and not a day goes by when I'm not sitting by her hospital bed. I'm honestly terrified that she's going to wake up and tell someone what I did to put her there!

Red Rope

There was a young woman who lived in a studio apartment. It was just one large room with her bed at one end and the front door at the other.

Recently, she had heard rumours about a series of murders that had taken place in the apartment building. All of the victims were young women, and they all lived alone. Each one had been strangled with a piece of red rope. Apparently, the killer left it wrapped around all their victims necks as a 'calling card'. The police had no idea who the killer was, or how they managed to convince the victims to let them into their apartments so late at night.

So the police put a notice up on the notice board in the main entrance of the building to warn its residents to always lock their doors and remain vigilant.

The landlord arranged to have all the locks in the building changed to more robust and secure locks.

Specific trades-people were brought in to check the locks on all the windows in the building.

Despite all the precautions that had been taken, the young woman was still very worried. Every night she made sure that her door and windows were securely locked, and left the lamp on throughout the night.

One night, just after 3am, she was woken up by a faint noise. By the light of the lamp, she was able to see that the doorknob on her front door was slowly turning. She knew that if she didn't do something fast, she would be killed! Thinking quickly, she grabbed a wooden chair and tiptoed over to the front door. As it slowly opened, she hid behind the door and waited. She was so scared that she held her breath for fear of being heard.

The shadowy figure of a man stepped into her apartment and as soon as she saw him, she brought the chair crashing down on his head. She hit him again and again until he stopped moving. The man was knocked unconscious, and she quickly raised the alarm by shouting for her neighbours to come and help her. Then she called the police.

When the police arrived, they took the mask off the unconscious man's head, and the young woman recognised him immediately. It was the landlord. In his pocket they found a piece of red rope, and a key ring that had a key to every apartment in the building.

> When the genie asked for my one and only wish, I replied "allow me to see through any surface". As I write this with my eyes closed, I feel sure that I should have ended that sentence with the words "at will".

50

The Guesthouse

A young man called Brian and his wife Louise were driving on a short holiday trip to the countryside. They set off a little later than they had planned, and it was starting to get a little late. Rather than getting lost along the winding roads of the countryside, they decided to look for a place to stay overnight and continue their journey in the morning.

Just off the road in the distance, they saw a small house by the side of woods.

"Maybe they rent rooms out there" said Louise.

So they both decided to stop and ask. When they knocked on the door, an elderly man and woman answered. The old man told the couple that while they didn't usually rent rooms out, they would be happy to have them as guests for the evening, and give them a bed to sleep in until the morning.

So Brian and Louise entered the old house, and the old woman made them each a cup of tea. Later she also brought them some cake from the kitchen. The four of them all had a good chat, before Brian and

Louise were taken to their room. They explained that they wanted to pay for the room and their hospitality, but the old man said that he would not accept any money from them.

The next morning, Brian and Louise were up early before their hosts had woken up. On a table in the kitchen near the back door, they left an envelope with some money in it for the room. Then they started making their way towards the next town.

On the way, they stopped at a small roadside cafe and had breakfast. When they told the cafe owner where they had stayed, and about the nice old couple who had invited them in, the owner turned pale and appeared shocked. "That can't be" he said. "That house burned down to the ground over 50 years ago, and the old man and woman who lived there died in the fire".

Both Brian and Louise could not believe it. Surely the owner was thinking of a different house. So they travelled back to the house, only this time, there was no house. All they found was a burned out shell surrounded and overgrown with weeds. They stood staring at the ruins trying to understand what had happened.

"Maybe this is the house that the restaurant owner was talking about, but it is a different house to the one we stopped in" said Louise.

"Yeah, I must have taken the wrong road on the way back" said Brian.

As they searched through the rubble, untouched for decades, they noticed a badly burned table towards the rear of the house. Resting on it was the envelope they had left there that morning.

➢ Never trust your own reflection in the mirror. It's the only thing in the world that could seamlessly replace you.

➢ While tidying my laboratory, I came across an unfamiliar notebook and opened the first page. It read 'Warning! The subject still thinks he is the scientist'.

51

Face to Face

A family went on holiday together and checked into a cheap, old hotel. They booked two rooms - a double room for the mother and father, and a single room for their young, teenage daughter.

When they all got to their rooms, the teenage daughter detected a bad odour in hers. The father called down to the front desk and asked to speak to the manager. He explained how his daughter's room smelled very bad, and they would like another room for her. The manager apologised and told the father that all the other rooms were booked because of a nearby festival, but agreed that he would send a maid up to his daughter's room to try and get rid of the odour.

After lunch, the family went back to their rooms. When the daughter walked into her room, she could still smell the bad odour. Again, her father called the front desk and told the manager that his daughter's room smelled really bad! The manager again apologised, but told him that there was little else they could do.

So the teenage daughter spent the night in the room. She held her breath, trying not to breathe in the dreadful odour. Eventually, she got to sleep, lying spread out on her front.

In the morning, her parent's knocked on her door to wake her up. When the daughter got up and opened the door, both of her parents immediately smelled the awful stink, and so the father decided that he had to get to the bottom of what was causing such a horrible smell. So he started searching the entire room for the source of the bad odour. He sniffed the towels, took down the curtains and checked the carpet. The mother and daughter helped too. They checked the bed sheets and the mattress. As the daughter pulled the thin, spongy mattress off the bed, she noticed that there was a big hole in the base underneath. She looked down into the base of the bed and saw a horrible sight.

There, lying face up inside the base of the bed was the decomposing and rotting body of a dead old man. The daughter then realised that she had been sleeping the whole night face-to-face and only inches away from a rotting corpse.

> After I asked the crystal ball to tell me how to escape death, I was very confused when it read 'No thanks honey, I'm full'. At that moment, my wife appeared from the kitchen offering me a slice of after dinner cake.

52

The Camera

There was a young boy called Anthony who was 15 years old. It was his father's birthday soon and he wanted to buy him something really nice. Unfortunately he didn't have very much money, so he decided to have a look around a local market.

While browsing through the stalls, Anthony spotted a little digital camera. He remembered that his father had always wanted one, so he picked it up and took a look at it. The camera was a bit old, and there were scratches and scuff marks on the outside, but when he looked through the viewfinder, everything was clear. Even though the camera was second-hand, it seemed in rather good condition.

To see if it worked, Anthony took a picture of a little wooden chair by the side of the stall. He asked the seller how much they wanted for it. The price was far cheaper than he had expected, so he immediately handed over the cash and bought it.

As he was leaving, the seller mentioned that the camera had once belonged to one of three college students who had mysteriously disappeared. Upon hearing this, Anthony felt a little unnerved.

He went to take another picture of the small wooden chair to make sure that it definitely worked, but the chair had since been moved, so he took a picture of the seller instead before quickly running off happy with his purchase.

A few days later, Anthony, his mother and his little brother waited anxiously for his father to arrive home from work. As soon as he opened the front door, they shouted "Happy Birthday!" and started giving him his presents. The digital camera was exactly what his father wanted. He went out into the garden to test out the camera and took a photograph of the family dog.

Later that afternoon, while everyone was in house drinking and enjoying the party, Anthony sat alone in the garden and examined the camera. He called for the family dog, but he was nowhere to be seen. He must have been inside the house receiving attention from someone else.

When examining the camera, Anthony noticed that there were still some other photos saved in its memory. He found that some of the pictures were of three young people, and wondered if these were the three college students who had mysteriously disappeared.

That was when it suddenly dawned on him. The camera was cursed! He had to tell his parents. He dropped the camera on the grass outside and ran inside the house.

"Dad! Dad! The camera is cursed!" cried Anthony. "Whatever it takes a picture of disappears!"

As Anthony raced back out into the garden, closely followed by his father and his mother, he was horrified to see his younger brother now playing with the camera. Quickly, he ran over and snatched it out of the little boy's hands.

"Did you take any pictures?" asked Anthony.

"Yes, but only one. Why?" replied his brother.

Anthony's heart sank.

"What did you take a picture of?" he asked.

"I took a picture of the sun" replied his brother.

Just then, it suddenly began to grow very dark...

➢ I didn't see the kid that usually waves at me on my waste disposal route today. As I dumped their household bin into the compactor, his mother came out and asked if her son scared me when he jumped out of the bin.

53

The Little Old Lady

The policeman sat on the sofa with his pen and notebook in his hands. The little old lady came in with a cup of tea and set it down on the table next to him.

"Before you take me down to the police station, perhaps I should tell you why I did it, Officer?" she said. "The truth is it was mostly for the company. It gets very lonely when you're an old lady, and young people never seem to want to spend any time with me. I just enjoy sitting and talking".

The policeman just stared at her impassively.

"Jessica was the very first" she said, as she sat down in her comfy armchair. "I remember it like it was yesterday. She came to my door selling cleaning products. I invited her inside and made her a cup of tea. Then I went to the kitchen to fetch my axe, and when she least expected it, I crept up behind her and chopped off her head!"

"The next was Daniel. He was an electrician and he came to fix my faulty lights. While he was taking a break from his work, I made him a cup of tea. Then I took my axe from behind the sofa and chopped his head off too!"

"The third one was Christopher. He was the milkman. I told him to come inside while I looked for my purse. I made him a cup of tea too, and as he sat down to drink his tea, I took my axe and chopped his head off too!"

"I stuffed all the heads and placed them on my mantelpiece. I talk to them, day and night. I carry on conversations with them. It really helps with the loneliness. The only problem was what to do with the bodies. I couldn't stuff them all - that would be too much work! So I came up with an ingenious solution".

"What did I do? Well it was simple. I simply stuffed one of the bodies and used it for all the heads. When I was tired of talking to one of them, I would take the head off, put it back on the mantelpiece, and then place another head on the body. Isn't that clever?"

The policeman didn't answer.

"Well, I'm getting a little bored with our conversation, Officer" said the little old lady, with a sigh. She then stood up, took the policeman's head, and put it back on the mantelpiece. Then she took the saleswoman's head and placed it on the body.

"Oh, good afternoon Jessica" she said. "It's so nice to see you again! How have you been?"

> "Just in case you're wondering, the tubes in your arm and nose will keep you alive and healthy for decades" she said with a smile, before nailing the coffin lid shut.

54

The Storage Room

There was a young, newly-married couple called Jennifer and Thomas who lived together in an old apartment building. Jennifer was a student at university studying psychology, and Thomas worked in construction on a nearby building site.

The young couple loved their new apartment and put a lot of effort into renovating and decorating it to really make it feel like their own home. The apartment was a good size and had a large living room, a kitchen, a bathroom and two good sized bedrooms. In the hallway, there was an ample storage room that was filled with all sorts of old junk.

One evening, Jennifer was preparing dinner and humming quietly to herself, while Thomas was in the living room sitting on the couch and watching the television. He remembered that one of the light bulbs in the main bedroom had gone out and that the bulb needed to be replaced.

The walk-in storage room in the hallway had cupboards and shelves. It was completely packed with paint cans, pieces of carpet, replacement door handles, cleaning products, candles, boxes of matches and other stuff. It was a very good sized storage room, and the couple kept all their bits and bobs in there. The spare light bulbs were in one of the drawers towards the back of the storage room.

As Thomas was moving through the junk to get to the light bulbs, he tripped over something and fell to the floor with a crash!

"Thomas, you're so clumsy!" shouted Jennifer from the kitchen. "Are you alright?"

She then heard the door to the storage room close.

"Yes, I'm alright" replied Thomas. "I just stumbled over all this junk you keep in here".

"Don't blame me" said Jennifer. "You're the one who decided to go poking around in there".

"I wanted to replace the light bulb in the bedroom" said Thomas.

"Okay, go ahead" said Jennifer, as she continued to cook dinner.

The following morning, when Jennifer woke up, Thomas had already left for work. So she took a shower, got dressed and hurried off to university for one of her classes.

When she arrived home that evening, Jennifer stopped at the front door of the apartment. Searching through her purse, she quickly realised that she had forgotten her keys. The door was locked and she didn't have any way to open it. Unfortunately, she had forgotten to bring her mobile phone as well, so she had to wait at the front door for her husband to arrive home from work.

She waited and waited, but Thomas never showed up! It was getting dark and Jennifer began to wonder what had happened to him. In frustration, she banged on the door with her fists.

All of a sudden, she heard a click and the door creaked open. She walked into the hallway, closed the door behind her and wearily dropped her backpack onto the floor.

When Jennifer looked into the living room, she stopped in her tracks. Thomas was sitting on the sofa watching the television.

"You mean you were at home all this time?" asked Jennifer, in frustration.

Thomas simply looked up at her and smiled.

Just then, something caught Jennifer's attention. "What's that smell?" she asked.

"I don't smell anything?" replied Thomas.

Jennifer wandered around the apartment sniffing and looking for the source of the putrid smell. The smell was the strongest in the hallway - it was so unpleasant, it made her feel nauseous. The door of the storage room was ajar, so Jennifer reached out, grasped the handle and pulled the door open.

She saw something that made her gasp in horror. Lying there on the floor of the storage room, surrounded by old junk, was the dead body of her husband, Thomas. He had hit his head on one of the corners of the drawers as he fell and had bled to death.

As she stared in horror, Jennifer heard the voice of her husband behind her asking "what's wrong, Jennifer?"

➢ We have found your missing husband, the officer said, as he drew an 'X' on the map - and then he drew another, and another, and another, and another, and another.

55

The Date

There was a young girl called Michelle who was 19 years old, and she was desperate to find herself a boyfriend. Everything in her life was perfect. She lived at home with her parents, who were happily married and had just passed their 23rd wedding anniversary. She had just started studying at university and was enjoying her course. She had a great group of friends that had fun together and supported each other when needed. She had everything in her life, except for that one nice, sweet young prince to love and to hold.

One day, Michelle was bored and decided to join an internet dating website. After fending off many inappropriate comments and suggestive messages from giggling 15-year-old boys and middle-aged, unhappily married men, she finally met a young man who she instantly liked!

He seemed to know all the right things to say. He seemed charming, thoughtful and romantic - far more mature and gentlemanly than any of the other boys she had talked to. They found that they had a lot in common. The website did not show any pictures, but from how they described one another, she felt an immediate attraction to him and his personality. She hoped that he felt equally the same for her.

Over the next few days they chatted online every chance they got. Michelle found herself gradually falling in love with him. As the weeks passed, their conversations became much more intimate, and Michelle decided that she simply had to meet this young man in person!

Michelle sent him a message proposing that they should take the next step and meet up at a local cafe for tea. The man messaged her back agreeing to meet and seemed enthusiastic about arranging a day and time.

He said that he would be wearing a brown jacket, so that she could easily identify him. Michelle told him that she would be wearing a red dress.

A few days later, Michelle walked into the cafe wearing a very provocative, low-cut and figure hugging red dress. Her heart was pounding with excitement at the anticipation of meeting her new prince charming.

Moments later a man wearing a brown jacket walked into the cafe and tapped Michelle on the shoulder. As she turned around to look at him, they both gasped in horror. "Michelle!" he yelled. "Daddy!" she cried.

- My housemates think that our house is haunted. I've lived here for over 213 years now and I've never seen or heard anything.

➢ I work at a crematorium loading bodies into the furnace. You would be surprised how many times you hear screams right after the furnace door closes!

The Psychic

There was a young woman who decided to visit a psychic, because she was curious about what life had in store for her. Although she didn't really believe in fortune telling, she thought it would be fun to have her future told.

The young woman arrived at the psychic's house and was greeted at the door by an old lady in ragged clothing. The psychic ushered her inside and led her down the hallway to a darkened room, where they both sat down at a table.

"Can you tell me my future?" asked the woman.

"Of course" replied the psychic. "Just show me your palm?"

The woman held out her hand and the psychic examined it carefully, frowning in concentration.

There was a long silence and the young woman began to feel uncomfortable. Suddenly, the psychic went very pale in the face and gave the woman a strange look.

"Is there something wrong?" asked the woman, nervously.

The psychic refused to answer any questions and told the woman that it was late she wanted the woman to leave. She added that there would be no charge for the reading.

The woman was very worried and began asking questions, but no matter how much she begged and pressed for answers, the psychic would not say a single word! As the woman kept insisting, the psychic just kept shaking her head while ushering her out of the house.

Finally, when the woman began to grow angry, the psychic relented. She took a pen and a piece of paper and wrote something down. She then folded it up, put it in an envelope and handed it to the woman.

"Do not read this until you get home tonight" the psychic told her.

The woman was relieved and stuffed the envelope into her pocket. She thanked the psychic and paid her for her services. They said their goodbyes and the woman left, thinking about the mysterious note and wondering what it could possibly say.

As the woman crossed the road, still deep in thought, she wasn't looking where she was going and walked right into the path of an oncoming truck. The vehicle slammed right into her, tossing her into the air like a rag doll. Her broken body flew and bounced along the road, finally coming to rest in a crumpled and motionless heap.

The police arrived and pronounced the poor woman dead on the scene. While searching through her pockets, looking for identification, one of the police officers came across the envelope.

When he opened it, the note read 'You have no future'.

- After so many years of living alone in this large, old house, I came to a startling revelation. During my time here, I have closed far more doors than I've opened!

57

The Guard Dog

A young girl lived alone in her house with only her dog to protect her. At night, she would close and lock all the doors, and close and lock all the windows, except for one. She always kept the bathroom window open to allow some fresh air into the house. Her dog would always take its place under her bed at night when she slept.

One evening, she sat down and had some supper, fed her dog and then decided to go to sleep for the night. Settling down, she snuggled up in bed and drifted off to sleep.

That night, she was awoken just after 2am by a scratching and whimpering sound coming from the bathroom. The girl was too scared to go and check it out, so she decided it must just be some noise coming from outside. She reached her hand down under her bed and felt the reassuring lick from her dog that allowed her to fall back to sleep.

A little later in the night, she was once again awoken by the sound of scratching and whimpering coming from the bathroom, so she reached her hand down under the bed to feel the reassuring lick of her dog, before falling back to sleep.

A short time later, once again, she was awoken by the sound of scratching and whimpering coming from the bathroom. She reached her hand down to feel the reassuring lick of her dog, and out of sheer curiosity, decided to go take a look at what was making those scratching and whimpering sounds.

She got out of bed and slowly walked towards the bathroom. As she approached the bathroom, the scratching and whimpering noises seemed to get louder and louder.

She turned the door handle to the bathroom, opened the door and reached out to switch on the light. What she saw shocked her!

The sounds were coming from her dog, which had been tied to the radiator and muzzled. Around her dog's collar was a note, that read 'Humans can lick too!'

➢ I often wondered what made my pillow so soft. When it accidently tore open one day, I stared in horror as millions of spiders quickly spread and ran all over my bed!

The Vault

Jake had a summer job working in a cemetery. It wasn't the type of work he would normally choose, but his dad was friends with the undertaker and had convinced him to take the job, despite his fear of dead bodies.

It was a very eerie place to work and after being there for over a week, Jake still got the creeps when he caught sight of a corpse. Luckily, he didn't have to get anywhere near the dead bodies.

His work consisted mostly of digging graves, cleaning and cutting the grass. His boss, the undertaker, was the one who prepared the dead bodies for burial.

The scariest things were the vaults. Families bought these large tombs and every member of their family who died was placed inside the vault inside a coffin. The thought of all those dead bodies lying around inside of these dusty chambers and secret rooms was very creepy to Jake.

Over time, Jake got used to working in the cemetery and everything was going well until, one evening, when the unthinkable happened.

While Jake was inside one of the vaults, sweeping the floor and polishing the name plates, a gust of wind blew the vault door shut. He realised that, to his horror, he was trapped inside of the vault and surrounded by dead bodies. There was no one around to help him and his worst nightmare had literally come true!

He shouted for help, but it was no use. The undertaker's house was too far away and no one could hear him. As the hours passed by, and feeling increasingly desperate, Jake realised that he would have to rely on himself, and so he began to think of a way out.

There was a small window high up above the vault door. Unfortunately, it was far too high for him to reach. Looking around the tomb, he decided that he could use the coffins. If he stacked them up, one on top of the other, they could form a flight of stairs for him to climb up to the window.

After stacking the coffins up against the door, Jake proceeded to climb up them very slowly while taking care not to tip them over. Just when he thought his plan was working, he stepped on the very top coffin and the wood gave way under his feet. His foot went straight through the coffin lid and he felt a sudden, sharp pain in his leg.

Crying out in agony, he could picture the splintered wood and rusty nails slicing into his skin. The stack of coffins began to wobble and for one horrifying moment, he thought that he was going to lose his balance and tumble down to the stone floor.

Luckily, he managed to grab onto the window and steady himself. He could feel the blood trickling down his leg. Despite the pain he was in, Jake pulled himself up and began shaking his leg to free himself from the coffin lid. The stack of coffins tipped over and clattered to the ground.

Clinging to the window, Jake pulled himself up and crawled through the narrow opening. He dropped down on the grass outside and limped towards the undertaker's house to get help.

The undertaker came out and found Jake lying on his doorstep clutching his bleeding leg. He carried the boy to his car and drove him straight to the hospital.

After the doctor had washed off all the blood, he started to examine Jake's wound.

"How did you get these injuries?" asked the doctor.

"I was cut by some broken pieces of wood" replied Jake.

"Well these aren't cuts" said the doctor. "They're human bite marks!"

➢ I was video chatting in bed with my husband, who was away on business, when I accidently dropped my mobile phone on the bedroom floor. As I reached to pick up it up, my husband's face changed - and as he held his finger to his lips indicating to be quiet, he wrote "There's someone under your bed!"

The Clown

There were two young teenage boys called Kevin and Martin who were best friends, and they loved watching horror movies together. One day a parcel had been left at the front door for Kevin. There were no stamps on the mysterious package, nor was there an address label - so Kevin could only assume that the parcel had been delivered by hand. Kevin was not expecting any deliveries, so he had no idea what it was or who it was from?

When he opened the parcel, he saw that it contained a DVD. There was no cover on the case, nor was there a title on the disc. He thought that one of his friends might be playing a prank on him, so he called his best friend Martin and asked him about the DVD. Martin had no idea about the mysterious DVD, but asked if he could come over to Kevin's house so that they could watch it for the first time together. Of course, Kevin agreed.

So Kevin and Martin sat down in Kevin's living room, while his parents were still at work, and pressed play on the DVD player.

What they saw really surprised them both. The recording showed a creepy and hideous looking clown standing in a room. The clown was standing close to the camera holding a large wooden mallet, and they could just see in the background a bed to his right, a wardrobe to his left and behind him a closet door.

The clown was just staring into the camera with an evil looking grin. He was holding the mallet with both hands, motioning the head of the mallet up and down, as if he was getting ready to smash something. Occasionally, the clown would point directly at the camera, so it appeared like it was pointing at Kevin and Martin.

Of course Kevin and Martin thought the video was hilarious, and they both started laughing out loud, while wondering who could have possibly left this at the front door for Kevin. They both came to the conclusion that it had been left at the wrong house, for the wrong 'Kevin', but they had no way of passing it on to the intended recipient.

Eventually the clown stopped, turned around and slowly opened the closet door that was behind him. As he entered, he turned around, grinned menacingly and closed the closet door.

At this moment Kevin stopped laughing. As Martin turned to look at him, he could see that Kevin's face was as white as a sheet, and his eyes were open wide in terror.

"What's the matter with you?" asked Martin. "Why aren't you laughing?"

"That's my bedroom" replied Kevin.

> I woke up to the sound of knocking on glass. At first I thought it was coming from my bedroom window, but then I realised it was coming from the mirror! When I got up and looked into the mirror, I saw my reflection blink.

60

The Unfrozen

Kenneth was a very wealthy man, but all the money in the world couldn't save him now. He was dying, and there was nothing more the doctors could do for him. They had all tried their best, but their best just wasn't good enough.

"We're going to freeze your body, Kenneth" said the doctor. "You will be placed in suspended animation. Hopefully, at some point in the future, medical science will have advanced far enough to heal you. In the meantime, your body will be cryogenically frozen and kept in storage".

When Kenneth woke up and opened his eyes, he found himself lying on a bed in an unfamiliar room. There was a man standing over him. A very tall man, dressed in a shimmering, silver robe.

"Welcome to the future" said the man.

Kenneth coughed and cleared his throat.

"Who are you?" asked Kenneth.

"I'm your descendant" replied the man. "You've been asleep for a very long time. You're my ancestor. It's a pleasure to meet you".

"What's your name?" asked Kenneth.

"My name is Locutus" replied the man, smiling.

"Locutus" said Kenneth. "That's a funny name".

"Not really" said Locutus. "Kenneth is infinitely more amusing".

"What do you do for a living?" asked Kenneth.

"Living?" replied Locutus, looking confused. "I don't understand the question. Oh, you mean work? No, we don't do that anymore. The robots do all the work now".

"How convenient" said Kenneth. "What year is it?"

"It's 27 ADL" replied Locutus.

"27 ADL. What on Earth does that mean?" asked Kenneth.

"27 years After our Dear Leader came to power" replied Locutus.

"Who's the Dear Leader?" asked Kenneth.

"Oh, he's our leader" replied Locutus, proudly. "He is the greatest leader the world has ever known. He single-handedly united all the countries on Earth. All hail the Dear Leader".

"Where are we?" asked Kenneth.

"We are in a bunker, approximately two miles beneath the surface of the Earth" replied Locutus. "Quite a change from your time, I would imagine. It's far too hot for anyone to live above ground now".

"Keeping me in storage all this time must have cost a fortune" said Kenneth. "Did my savings cover it?"

"I'm afraid not" replied Locutus. "Your savings ran out about 15 years ago. I had to pay all your debts when I had you revived".

"Well, thank you" said Kenneth. "That was very kind of you".

"Think nothing of it" said Locutus, with a smile. "It was my pleasure".

Kenneth then tried to get up, but he was too dizzy and instead, he slumped back down on the bed with a groan.

"You must not move" said Locutus. "You need to rest for the heart transplant".

"Oh" said Kenneth. "Is there something wrong with my heart?"

"No" replied Locutus. "There's something wrong with mine".

➢ I found a dead body in the boot of my car today, which is strange, because I remember putting two in there yesterday!

➢ I think I might be the most successful serial killer in history. The best part is telling their loved ones that we did everything we could.

Top Brands

There was a 17 year old boy called Oliver who was obsessed with brand named clothing, and he simply refused to wear anything that wasn't a top named brand! Every item of clothing he owned - shirts, t-shirts, jumpers, jackets, ties, belts, jeans, trousers, underwear, shoes and trainers - were all brand named clothing.

His parents spoiled him terribly and bought him everything he wanted! They both worked very hard in order to earn enough money to satisfy their son's expensive tastes. It had been years since they had bought any clothes for themselves. However, Oliver was selfish and never appreciated the sacrifices they made for him.

One day he told them that he needed a new pair of trainers. That evening, they returned home from the local department store and handed him a bag. Oliver snatched the bag from their hands without even a 'thank you'. When he opened it and looked inside, he suddenly flew into a fury!

"You idiots!" he shouted angrily. "How could you be so stupid?"

"What's wrong, Oliver?" asked his mother, timidly. "What's wrong? Are they the wrong size?"

Oliver was seething with anger. "Useless!" he shouted. "These are the wrong colour! I asked for red, and these are white! I specifically said RED!"

"Couldn't you just try these ones on?" asked his father. "Perhaps you will like them on?"

Boiling with rage, Oliver picked up one of the trainers and slapped his father across the face with it. "Rubbish!" he shouted. "I said RED, not white!

You expect me to wear white trainers, do you? I wouldn't be caught dead in these things. Take them away and burn them!" He then threw the trainers at his parents and slammed his bedroom door shut.

The next day Oliver, reluctantly, decided to try on the new white trainers and go for a walk to see how they felt. While they were comfortable, he cursed his parents for how stupid and inconsiderate they were for not buying him the right colour trainers - he wanted RED trainers!

During his walk, Oliver came across a railway line and could see that a train was approaching in the distance. As he stepped across the track, his laces became entangled in the rails, and he tripped and fell onto the tracks.

Frantically trying to untangle his laces from the tracks, Oliver looked up just in time to see the train bearing down on him before it ran straight across his legs and cut his feet off at the ankles!

A horrified policeman who witnessed this from a distance hurried over and immediately called an ambulance. The terribly injured boy was rushed immediately to hospital. He was bleeding profusely, and while the doctors were unsure whether he would make it, they were able to slow the bleeding and stabilise his condition.

After the ambulance had left, the policeman went out onto the tracks. He collected Oliver's trainers and dropped them into a plastic bag. Oliver's feet were still inside the trainers, which had been completely saturated and stained a very vibrant blood red.

> "Please, take me instead!" I screamed, while grabbing at the two men who took my child. "Sorry lady, children only" they said, as they finished loading up the last lifeboat on the ship.

The Button

A husband and wife were sitting at home one evening when they heard a knock at the door. When they opened the door there was a strange gentleman standing on the doorstep. He was dressed in an expensive black suit and was holding a large briefcase.

"I wonder if I might have a moment of your time?" asked the gentleman.

Assuming that he was a travelling salesman, the couple invited him inside.

The gentleman placed his briefcase down on the living room table and took something out. It was a little black box with a single red button on the top. He handed the box to the husband and wife.

"Today is your lucky day" said the gentleman, in a calm tone. "You have the opportunity to become rich beyond your wildest imagination! If you press this button, you will receive £1,000,000 in cash. There is just one catch - someone you don't know will die".

The gentleman then opened his briefcase to reveal stacks of money inside! He told the couple that he would return the following day, at the same time, to retrieve the black box - so they had 24 hours to decide if they wanted to press the button.

After he left, the husband and wife discussed the box and whether or not to press the button. They talked for hours, weighing up the opportunity to have £1,000,000 cash and all the fun and financial security this would offer, against the ethical and moral aspect of killing an unknown and unseen stranger.

Eventually, they both agreed to press the button. On the count of 3, 2, 1, they both pressed their fingers down on the button at the same time.

Nothing happened.

The next day, the gentleman returned at the same time, just as he had promised, and he took back the little black box. He then poured £1,000,000 in cash from his briefcase onto their living room table.

The couple were ecstatic - they held the bundles of money in their hands laughing and smiling knowing they had a much brighter future ahead of them!

As the gentleman was about to leave, the husband asked him "so, did someone really die?"

"Of course" replied the gentleman. "It happened last night. In some distant and far away place, someone you don't know died".

Both the husband and wife felt guilty, but as they turned to look at all the money spread across the table, they could not do anything but smile.

"Just one more question" said the husband.

"Yes, of course, what do you want to know?" asked the gentleman.

"What are you going to do with that little black box now?" asked the husband.

The gentleman just smiled and replied "I'm going to give it to someone who doesn't know you".

> "Officer, I just looked away for a second and my baby was gone!" I sobbed, helplessly. "That's better - I sounded much more convincing that time" I thought with a smile, as I finally picked up the phone to call the police.

63

The Parents

There was a young girl called Alice who wanted to attend a nightclub for the very first time. She asked her parents for permission, but they said that she was too young. When she argued with them, they refused to listen to her and sent her to her room.

The girl was very angry and decided to sneak out of the house. She really wanted to go to the nightclub! So she took some pillows and placed them under the blankets on her bed, so it looked like she was sleeping there. Then she got dressed, put on some makeup and slowly opened her bedroom door. She could hear her parents talking in the kitchen downstairs, so she gently closed her bedroom door, opened her bedroom window, climbed down onto the garage roof below, and was able to climb her way down onto the top of the car that was parked to the side of the garage.

When she got home later that night, she climbed back in through her bedroom window and found that her bed had been disturbed. When she looked closer she noticed that the blankets were all crumpled, but they were also ripped as if they had been cut.

In the morning, when Alice came down for breakfast, she didn't say anything to her parents. She could see that they were looking at her strangely though.

Later that evening, Alice wanted to call one of her friends, but she had run out of credit on her mobile phone. She told her parents that she was going out to the local shop to top up her mobile phone credit, and her parents told her that they were going out for dinner.

It was getting dark and on her way back, Alice had to walk through a park. As Alice was walking down a deserted pathway, all of a sudden a masked man jumped out of the bushes and tried to attack her! He had a long, iron bar in his hand and swung it right at her. She managed to dodge the iron bar as it flew past her head. Alice immediately fled before the masked man could catch her. She ran just as fast as she could, not daring to look back until she arrived back home.

Alice's parents arrived home just a few minutes later and the terrified Alice told them what had happened. They told her to be more careful in the future, and suggested that she take a long, hot bath to relax and calm her nerves. So Alice got herself undressed and got into the bath. She shut her eyes and tried to forget about the disturbing events of the day.

Suddenly the door flew opened and her mother came rushing in with a toaster. Before Alice had a chance to react, her mother tried to throw the toaster into the bathtub. However, her mother had misjudged the length of the wire and the toaster couldn't reach that far. The wire stopped the toaster short of landing in the bathtub and it dropped harmlessly onto the bathroom floor. Alice had only narrowly escaped being killed by an electric shock!

Jumping out of the bath, Alice started screaming at her parents. In that moment she realised that they had been trying to kill her all along! The knife marks through the blankets, the masked assailant and now this - it all started to make sense!

Grabbing her mobile phone, Alice told her parents that she would call the police immediately, unless they told her why they wanted her dead. Her mother burst into tears and her father hung his head in shame. Her parents sat down on the edge of the bath and tried to explain.

It turned out that Alice's uncle, her father's brother, was terminally ill in hospital. He was a very successful businessman and had amassed a huge fortune during his long career. He had no children of his own, so when he drew up his will, he decided to leave all his wealth to his favourite little niece.

When the uncle died, Alice would receive over £5,000,000. If Alice died first, then the money would automatically go straight to her parents.

Alice couldn't believe what her parents were telling her. She realised in that moment that her parents were both incredibly greedy and soulless! She struggled to understand how her own parents could try to murder their own daughter for money. It was a betrayal that could never be forgiven!

Alice immediately packed all of her belongings and left the house that very night. She booked into a cheap hotel and decided to cut off all communication with her parents. Despite the many difficulties that she faced, she tried to make a life for herself on her own.

She eventually got a job and earned enough money to study at university. Although she was very busy working and studying, she always set aside some time each week to visit her uncle in hospital.

In her first year of university she met a young man in her class who seemed very nice and polite. He was quite good-looking and had a charming personality. He was kind, gentle and always made sure he was there for her in times of need. When she was in his arms, she always felt safe and protected. Finally, she had found someone in her life that she could trust.

A few months passed and the happy couple decided to get married. They had a modest wedding at a local church and invited all of their friends to celebrate the joyous occasion. However, Alice insisted that they not invite her parents to the wedding!

The day after the wedding, the newlyweds went on their honeymoon. Alice's husband had booked a short holiday at a scenic resort in the mountains right next to a beautiful lake. When they arrived, the location looked so beautiful and they decided to take a boat trip on the lake to take in the view. It was autumn and the leaves were falling from the trees. The sun was setting and casting a red glow across the skies and the resort was almost deserted.

When they rowed out to the centre of the lake, the husband stood up and took hold of Alice in his arms. He kissed her passionately, before pushing her over the side of the boat. Alice tumbled into the icy water with a splash. He grabbed an oar and began beating her over the head with it as she struggled to stay afloat. Eventually, he knocked her unconscious and she sank beneath the water. Then, he rowed back to the shore and called the police, tearfully recounting how his wife had accidently fallen overboard, banged her head and drowned.

A few days later, Alice's uncle was found dead in his hospital bed. He had been smothered with a pillow.

Within a few months Alice's parents received over £5,000,000 in inheritance from Alice's uncle, and they split it with Alice's ex-husband, as had been agreed.

> A few hours after realising I had been buried alive, I was thrilled to hear the sound of someone digging me out. My joy quickly turned

to terror when I realised the digging and scratching was coming from underneath the coffin!

64

The Stairs

When I was a child, I would race to the top of the stairs just as fast as I could. It was sort of a silly little game I played with myself. Well, I must have been only six or seven at the time. I'm not sure how old exactly, but I know that I was very young.

Somewhere along the way, I began hearing a voice at the top of the stairs whispering to me. It sounded like a man's voice and it would make bets with me.

"I bet you can't make it to the top of the stairs" it would whisper to me.

I wondered if it was just my imagination playing tricks on me. I was frightening myself and hearing this 'made up' voice that would 'get me' if I didn't make it up in time.

Well, I wasn't going to take a chance. I was too young to understand. I don't even think there was a certain amount of time that I had to get up there by - I just knew that I had to run up the stairs as fast as I possibly could!

Eventually the voice started to raise the stakes. Instead of pennies, it began to say things like "I bet you a good night's sleep that you can't make it to the top of the stairs".

Some time later it would say things like "I bet you your life that you can't make it to the top of the stairs".

Every single time I was terrified, and even though I knew it was just my imagination and my mind playing tricks on me, I could never take the chance and just ran up those stairs as quickly as I could every time.

However, as I got older, it stopped. I never really thought much about it at all. It was just some silly thing I did as a child. I never mentioned it to anyone, until one night when I was sleeping over at my brother's house.

We were telling spooky stories, and out of nowhere, I brought up the voice at the top of the stairs.

My brother suddenly became very quiet. Before I could tell him anything more about it, he asked me "did it make bets with you?"

We both looked at each other in horror!

> My sister lost her short-term memory in the car crash that killed her husband and three children. Every day she has to find out from me that her husband and three children are dead - and it feels better every time I do it!

The Intruder

It was very late and I was in the bedroom trying to rest. I changed the channel on the television and saw that the local news was on. Just then, there was a breaking news alert.

"Murderer on the loose" it said. "Police are warning everyone to be on the alert. Suspect is armed and highly dangerous".

I was just getting myself relaxed when suddenly I heard a strange noise downstairs. It sounded like someone had entered the house!

At that moment, my heart began beating faster and I broke out into a cold sweat. Straining my ears to listen, I thought I heard another noise. It was the sound of footsteps and a door creaking.

It wasn't my imagination - there was someone in the house! "I have to get out of here, fast!" I thought. So I slipped off the bed, as quietly as possible, and crept towards the window. My body was shaking with fear and I was trying not to make any noise.

Just then, I heard footsteps making their way up the stairs, and it sounded like more than one person. At any second, they would burst through the door. I had to get away!

I climbed out of the bedroom window and onto the garage roof, moving as fast as I could without making a noise. At the edge of the roof, I grabbed the drainpipe and lowered myself down until I dropped into the garden. As I paused, I looked up at the window I had just escaped from and saw the lights go on.

"That was close!" I thought, as a sudden chill ran down my spine thinking about what might have happened if they had caught me?

Without hesitation, I made my way to the bottom of the garden and ran into the woods. Once I was safely hidden by the trees, I broke into a fast run while stumbling through the darkness and the undergrowth, until I came to another housing estate.

Clutching my knife, which was still stained red with blood of the one occupant I found in the previous house, I headed on towards my next house.

- I decided to kill off a few characters in the book I'm writing. It will definitely spice up my autobiography a little.

- When I finally grabbed her in the darkness, I swam back to the surface. It never occurred to me how quickly the ice would freeze over!

66

Shared Custody

When my husband and I got divorced, I started living in a cheap, old and run-down apartment until I could get myself back on my feet. We shared custody of our daughter Sheila, so one week she would stay with me, and the next she would stay with my ex husband. She was only six years old at the time, so she didn't really understand everything that was going on.

One Saturday night, shortly after midnight, I was working on my computer researching the housing market. The computer desk was in the kitchen facing a wall, and on that same wall was the doorway that led to the bedrooms. So if Sheila got out of bed to get something from the kitchen, then she would have to walk right past me.

Sheila was always getting up during the night and getting herself into mischief. She would raid the fridge or knock something over while climbing over things. She liked to get up during the night to raid the fridge, or play around in the apartment, because she knew that I would likely be asleep and she could get away with it.

So while I was working on my computer I saw Sheila, in my peripheral vision, trying to sneak into the kitchen. She suddenly froze when she saw me. She just stood there looking right at me. I didn't look directly at her or pay her any attention. I figured that she had seen me, and that she knew she had been caught, so hopefully she would just go back to bed and go to sleep without me having to make a big deal of it.

Sheila continued to stand there for a few minutes, and I could see her the whole time, but I made a point not to look at her so that she would just go back to bed. She eventually turned and walked back towards her bedroom. It was dark in the room, with only the computer screen and the natural moonlight to illuminate the room, but I could still see her turn and leave.

After about 20 minutes, I got the feeling that I needed to go and check on her, because she was being too quiet and might be up to mischief in her room. In those 20 minutes, I should have heard her climb back into bed or playing in her room. Hearing absolutely nothing normally meant she was trying to be quiet for a reason! I think every parent gets that feeling occasionally when their child is up to mischief, and I got that feeling, so I got up to go and check on her.

I stood and walked into the hallway that led to the bedrooms. It was pitch black and I couldn't see a thing. This was the moment that, what had previously slipped my mind, suddenly hit me.

Sheila was staying with my ex husband that night - and not with me.

➢ A farmer tried to stop people stealing watermelons from his field by placing a sign up saying 'Warning! One of these watermelons has been injected with poison'. The next morning, someone had written on the bottom of the sign 'Now there are two!'

Little Red Pills

My husband has been a blessing to me since I got sick. I've seen so many doctors and specialists, but none of them can pinpoint exactly what's wrong with me. My doctor prescribed me some medicine to take every four hours. It's supposed to help me with the pain.

My husband is an excellent nurse. He's so very patient with me. At first I hated how he had to spend so much of his time looking after me. My illness was turning me into someone I didn't even recognise. I was becoming increasingly moody, temperamental and very impatient with him, but my husband just kept on going, giving me two of those little red pills every four hours to ease my pain.

For all that my husband was able to do for me, my symptoms began to worsen. My husband told me that he had left a message with the doctor, but as yet there had been no response. I started to get frequent nose bleeds and aching all over my body. It felt like I was slowly withering away and dying.

Apparently, the doctor feels that by increasing the frequency of my medication, this may help with my symptoms and the pain they cause me. So now my husband brings my medication to me once every two hours. I smile pitifully at my husband, thanking him for his devotion as I swallow those two little red pills.

He always sat by my bedside to make sure that I was taking my medication correctly, and would run his hand through my hair, that is, until large chunks of my hair started coming out in his hand.

I cried and cried, but I really just needed to be alone at that point, so I sent my husband out to the supermarket to get some essentials.

A few minutes after he had left, I suddenly realised that I was due to take another dose of my medication. So I weakly climbed out of bed and made it across to the bathroom and into the medicine cabinet. There were my little red pills scattered loosely around the cabinet. My husband must have knocked one of the bottles over without realising.

I grabbed the pill bottle that had been prescribed to me by my doctor. It had all the official labelling with my name written on it. When I unscrewed the lid of the pill bottle to put all the scattered pills back inside the bottle, I noticed that the pills in the bottle were white.

> Leaving the dying world infested with zombies behind, I managed to teleport to a time before it all started. Happy to now be living in a zombie-free world, I suddenly felt an aching pain in my left leg - and saw that the little scratch I had got from a zombie was now all red and infected.

68

Family Portraits

There was a man who decided to go rambling in the woods near where he lived. As night fell, he found himself in an unfamiliar part of the forest. He walked and walked, but he couldn't find his way home. Wandering aimlessly in the dark for what seemed like hours, he eventually came to a small clearing where an old, ramshackle cabin stood. Tired and weary, he decided to see if he could stay there for the night.

When he came closer to the cabin, he saw that the door was slightly ajar. Poking his head inside, he could see that the little cabin was completely empty, but there was a bed and a fire burning in the fireplace.

The man threw himself on the bed and decided to sleep there for the night. If the owner came back, he would apologise and explain how he came to be lost in the woods.

Lying on the bed and feeling exhausted, he looked around the cabin and was surprised to see the walls decorated with paintings. They appeared to be family portraits, all framed and painted in incredible detail. They seemed very life-like and, without exception, each family portrait was uglier than the last. The hideous faces in the pictures made him feel incredibly uneasy. The way they were painted, their faces were all twisted into looks of hatred and malice, and it seemed like their eyes were staring directly at him! It was all very unnerving.

He decided that the only way he was going to get any sleep was to ignore the hideous faces staring at him. So he turned on his side, facing the wall, pulled the blanket over his head and drifted off to sleep.

In the morning, the man woke up to find the cabin bathed in sunlight. When he looked up, he discovered that there were no family portraits on the walls of the cabin - only windows where the paintings had been.

> My husband keeps trying to convince me that our son passed away three years ago. As we argue, I feel a tug on my dress and a small voice asks me "who are you talking to, mummy?"

Text Messages

I have been dating my girlfriend for just over a year now. She is a wonderful person and has always been the light of my life. She has her little quirks of course, but who doesn't? These are the things that make us the people that we are, right?

One of her little quirks is her 'sleep texting'. She is a very heavy sleeper and I will often wake up in the morning to two or three text messages from her. Most of the time it's just a garbled message of auto-corrects and letters jumbled into nonsensical words. That was until last night anyway.

It was around 2am when I was awoken by my mobile phone vibrating on my bedside table. I rolled over and picked up my phone to see that I had received a text message from my girlfriend. A part of me thought about not even looking at it and just going back to sleep, but I just couldn't do that, knowing that there was a text message there from her. The paranoid and anxiety driven part of me wanted to know if something was wrong, so I decided to open the text message.

"Alexander" it read.

I found this particularly odd for several reasons. One being that the message actually made decent sense. I mean it was my name after all. Another, however, was that my girlfriend always called me Alex and not Alexander. Only my mother ever called me that! My curiosity got the better of me and I decided to respond.

I wrote back to her "Are you alright?" to which she almost immediately replied "Help me!"

When I received this reply, the hair stood up on the back of my neck, and I felt a cold shiver run down my spine. I immediately stood up, got changed and got into my car. It was only a short drive to her house, but it felt like hours! I decided to phone her on the way to her house.

Ring, ring, ring, ring, ring...

The line finally connected. On the other side I couldn't hear anything but heavy breathing. I said hello several times and called out her name, as panic and fear overwhelmed me.

Then I heard something. I heard the sound of feet shuffling around and then a deep, menacing giggle. Unsure who was on the other end of the line, I screamed into the phone demanding to know who I was speaking to, but it was too late. They hung up. Was I talking to my girlfriend in her sleep? Did someone have my girlfriend's phone?

Just then I turned the corner and arrived at my girlfriend's house. I pulled to a screeching halt on her driveway and ran towards the front door. Fortunately we shared copies of each other's house keys, so I let myself in and ran up the stairs to her room expecting a horrible scene.

What I saw as I burst through her bedroom door shocked me. There she was, just lying there in her bed sleeping. I slowly walked towards her and gently woke her up. As she awoke, she was surprised to see me. I asked her if she was alright and she replied "yes" in a rather surprised voice.

I checked her phone and there were the text messages she had sent to me, and the phone call she had taken from me while I was driving over.

Just to be sure, I checked underneath her bed and all around the house, but didn't find anything out of the ordinary.

My girlfriend must have sent the text messages and taken my call in her sleep. It was all very strange, but she had displayed some unusual behaviour in her sleep before, and I now knew she was safe and well. I stayed with her for about an hour, as she put her head back down on the pillow and fell back into a deep sleep almost immediately.

Once my panic and anxiety had calmed down, I stood up from her bed and showed myself out of her house. As I walked down the driveway towards my car, I ran through everything that had just occurred over and over in my mind.

The drive home still seemed to take longer than usual, as my mind raced over all the possible scenarios that could have played out. As I pulled into my driveway, I felt the vibration of my phone in my pocket. Fear once again crept up on me as I opened the text message from my girlfriend.

"You forgot to check the closet" it read.

> After struggling desperately to move any part of his paralytic body to alert the doctors that he was conscious before they made the first incision, he was relieved to see that one of the nurses had noticed his pupils dilating from the bright light. She leaned in close and whispered "you think we don't know that you're awake?"

Hell

There was a man who had lived a very bad life. One day he was killed in a car accident and was sent directly to Hell. Of course, the Devil was waiting for him!

"Welcome to Hell" said the Devil. "Now you must decide how you are going to spend eternity. There are three doors to choose from".

So the Devil took the man to the first door and opened it. Inside there were hundreds of people standing on their heads on a cement floor.

"That looks uncomfortable" said the man. "Let's see what's behind door number two?"

They moved onto the second door and the Devil opened it. Inside there were hundreds of people standing on their heads, but this time it was on a wooden floor.

"That looks uncomfortable too" said the man. "Show me what's behind door number three?"

So the Devil took him to the third door and opened it. Inside there were hundreds of people standing around chatting and drinking tea, but they were all up to their knees in poop!

"Hmm" said the man. "That looks bad, but it's better than the other two. I choose the third door!"

The Devil smiled and the man went into the third room and poured himself a cup of tea. Just as the door was closing behind him, he heard the Devil shout "okay people, tea break is over, now get back on your heads!"

➢ My daughter won't stop crying and screaming throughout the night. I visit her grave and ask her to stop, but nothing ever changes.

➢ With my one and only wish, I asked the genie for four walls and a roof above my head. I woke up in a coffin!

71

Hit and Run

It was 11pm and Stuart had been sitting in his dark living room for some time. He hadn't moved for hours! The terrible accident earlier that evening just kept playing over and over in his mind. The light had already turned to red, but he was in a hurry and accelerated through the red light long after it had changed.

Suddenly the object came into sight on his right hand side and in a split second, there was an almighty crash, before the biker rolled across his car bonnet and fell out of sight onto the pavement. Stuart, in a frenzied panic, put his foot straight down on the accelerator and screeched away from the chaos into the darkness. Shaken and in shock, he kept an eye on his rear-view mirror the whole way home.

"Why did you speed off, you idiot?" asked his wife, after he had explained to her what happened.

Stuart had never committed a crime before in his life. He sat there punishing himself by imagining years in jail, his career gone, his family gone and his entire future gone.

"Why not just go to the police right now?" asked his wife. "You can afford a lawyer".

Suddenly there was a firm tapping on the front door, and Stuart's world suddenly came crashing down.

"They've found me" said Stuart.

There was nothing he could do but answer the door. Running would only make matters worse! His body trembling, Stuart got up, walked across to the front door and opened it. A police officer stood in front of him.

"Would you happen to be Stuart?" asked the police officer.

"Yes, I'm Stuart" he replied, as he let out a defeated sigh. Please let me explain..."

The Policeman interrupted him abruptly.

"I am terribly sorry" said the police officer, "but I'm afraid I have some very bad news. Your son's bike was struck by a hit-and-run driver earlier this evening and he died at the scene. Had the driver stopped to assist the young man and called for an ambulance, it is almost certain he would have been saved. I am very sorry for your loss".

➤ I have a recurring nightmare where an intruder enters my home and murders my wife and my children. I would feverishly awake in a frightened panic with sweat-soaked sheets - except this morning, the sheets are bloody and there's a knife in my hand!

72

The Clown Doll

There was a wealthy married couple who lived in a large house and had two young children, a boy and a girl. After taking care of their children all week, both the mother and father decided that they needed a break, so they booked a table for an evening meal at a nice restaurant.

That evening, they called a young teenage girl they knew and trusted called Susan and arranged for her to come over and babysit their children while they were out. When Susan arrived, the parents told her to sort out supper for the children and put them to bed.

"After that, you can just watch the television and help yourself to anything in the fridge" said the father.

"Also, if you wouldn't mind, could you watch the television in our bedroom" said the mother. "The children have been having nightmares recently, so if you hear them crying, you can just go and calm them down".

Susan happily agreed and the parents left for their evening meal at the restaurant. Susan gave the children some milk and cookies and then ushered them upstairs to bed. She started to read them a bedtime story, and before long, both the little boy and girl were fast asleep. After tucking them in, she switched off the light and went to watch the television.

When Susan walked into the bedroom belonging to the parent's and sat down, she noticed there was a very creepy and evil-looking clown doll sitting in the corner of the room, just behind the bedroom door. As she watched the television she tried to ignore it, but it just sat there grinning at her. It looked so menacing and disturbing that it sent a chill down her spine. She felt as though its eyes were staring right at her as she sat there watching the television.

As time passed, Susan began to feel more and more uneasy about the clown doll. Whenever she glanced at it, she got the unsettling feeling that it had moved ever so slightly. Finally the clown doll began to freak her out so much that she couldn't stand it any longer.

She decided to go downstairs and phone the parents. When she dialled the number they had left for her, the father answered.

"Hello, it's me" said Susan. "Everything's fine. The children are fast asleep in bed. I was wondering though, would it be alright if I watched the television downstairs?"

"Of course" replied the father. "Why is that though?"

"Well, I know this sounds silly" replied Susan, "but the clown doll in your room is really creeping me out!"

"The clown doll?" asked the father.

"Yes, the clown doll in your bedroom" replied Susan.

The phone went silent for a moment.

"Listen to me very carefully" said the father. "Take the children and get out of the house. We will call the police. Go now!"

"What's wrong?" asked Susan.

"The children have been having nightmares, or so we thought, about a clown doll that keeps coming into their room in the middle of the night and watches them sleep" replied the father, "but we don't own a clown doll!"

> When I was a young child, I used to talk to my imaginary friend called Lucifer. That was until I told him to go away because he was doing bad things that I got the blame for. Tonight, 30 years later and still living at my childhood home, my 3 year old tells me she has a new best friend called 'Lucifer'.

The Farm

"Where are you?" I shrieked, as I ran through the abandoned farm. I can't find her. Not in the old house. Not in the old barn. I ran into the empty field, and I could feel my heart racing!

As I was running and scanning the area, I ran into a mound of dirt and tripped over, sprawling to the ground. Getting up, it suddenly hit me. It's an abandoned farm, but I trip over some freshly dug up soil - how can that be?

Crouching down, I started frantically clawing at the loose soil with my hands. After scooping handful after handful of the soil, I eventually hit something hard. Something wooden!

"Are you in there?" I cried out, while pressing my ear against the wood.

All I could hear were muffled cries coming from behind the wood. I continued digging, but soon I began to realise that it was taking far too long! Looking around, I saw a garden shed nearby. I sprinted towards it, ripping the door open. I saw a shovel, still caked in dirt. It was probably the same one that freak buried her with!

Running back, I started digging with purpose, faster and faster. Soon the wooden box was completely exposed. I tossed the shovel to one side and ripped open the crate. The girl stared back at me, eyes wide, bound and gagged, but alive! I had found her, thankfully, as I sighed in relief.

I reached into my bag and pulled out my rag and bottle of chloroform. I crouched down towards her and placed the rag over her face. "This will calm her down" I said to myself. She struggled and then quickly fainted. She was safe, as she lay there sleeping peacefully.

I then threw her over my shoulder, just as my brother appeared to me from wherever he had been hiding.

"Oh well!" said my brother, as I walked back to the truck with a smirk. "You found her".

"Yeah, you almost had me though!" I said, laughing.

My brother and I then sat down and had our lunch, before my brother took an afternoon nap.

"Okay, my turn" said my brother, once he had woken up. "Where did you hide her?"

I gestured towards the river area.

"Somewhere over there!" I replied with a smile, as my brother ran off to find her. "Drowning could be a problem though if you don't hurry up!"

> I framed the first letter I ever received as a police officer from a woman thanking me after I supported her through her husband's suicide. I passed it in my hallway every day for nearly ten years, before realising that the handwriting was the same as on her husband's suicide note.

74

The Apartment

Shaun had just finished his evening meal and was getting ready for bed. He was trying to get used to his new apartment, because it was the first time he had ever lived alone. Shaun was 25 years old, had been through university and had finally saved up enough money to afford a place of his own.

It was just after midnight, and after spending most of the day moving his belongings into his new apartment, Shaun lay down in his cosy bed. Just as he was slowly drifting off to sleep, he heard voices that seemed to be coming from the floor above him. It sounded like the voices of a man and a woman.

At first they were talking softly, but then it got louder and louder. They seemed to be arguing with each other. Shaun had to get up for work the next morning, and after an exhausting day, he needed all the sleep he could get! So he put the pillow over his head and tried to block out the noise, but the voices seemed to seep through.

Finally, when the voices started shouting at each other, Shaun couldn't take it anymore. So he got out of bed, took a broom from the kitchen and banged the tip of it against the ceiling. However, that didn't stop the voices, and by now they were arguing so loudly that the woman let out a long, blood-curdling scream.

"Stop shouting!" cried Shaun. "Some people have to get up early for work in the morning!"

Suddenly, the voices stopped. Just like that. There was an eerie silence. Shaun was satisfied and went back to bed. Once he had got himself settled and was feeling warm and comfortable, he slowly drifted off to sleep.

Unfortunately, the very next night around the same time, the voices started up again. The man's voice boomed loudly and the woman's shrill screech drowned him out. They were shouting over each other, but Shaun couldn't make out what either of them was saying. Now he was really angry! So as the couple were once again shouting and screaming at each other, he groggily climbed out of bed, took the broom and jabbed the ceiling once again with all his might.

As the woman once again let out another long, blood-curdling scream, Shaun shouted towards the ceiling "stop screaming! I'll call the police right now if you don't knock it off!"

Once again, the voices just suddenly stopped. He began to wonder why the voices died down so quickly when he shouted at them, but as long as he could get some sleep, he was happy.

When the very same thing happened for the third night in a row, Shaun decided that he'd had enough! He grabbed the phone on his bedside table and called the apartment manager to file a complaint against the noisy couple in the apartment above him.

His call was answered after the fifth ring.

"Hello" said the manager, in a tired voice.

"Hello, sir" said Shaun. "I'm sorry for calling you so late at night, but I have a complaint".

"Which is?" asked the manager, in a weary voice.

"The people in the apartment above me are constantly shouting and screaming at each other" replied Shaun. "I have a job and I have to be up early in the morning, but I can't sleep with them two screaming like that!"

"Alright" said the manager, "tell me your apartment number and I'll send someone over to speak with them in the morning".

Shaun gave the manager his apartment number, which was followed by a long silence on the other end of the line.

"Are you sure this is the correct information?" asked the manager, in a strange tone.

"Of course I'm sure" replied Shaun. "I know my own address!"

There was another long silence.

"You said the shouting was coming from the apartment above you, right?" asked the manager.

"Yes" replied Shaun, getting increasingly annoyed with the questions.

"That seems highly unlikely" said the manager, sounding rather confused. "You know, I've been the manager here for many years. I know the history of this building. About 50 years ago, a couple got into an argument at a party and, just after midnight, they took their argument up to the rooftop to get away from the guests. While they were up there, their argument intensified and the man ended up pushing his wife off the top of the building. She screamed all the way down to her death".

"What on Earth has that got to do with me?" asked Shaun.

"Well, your apartment is on the top floor" replied the manager. "There are no other apartments above yours".

- As I was tucking my son into bed, he said to me "daddy, please check for monsters under my bed?" So I looked under his bed and I saw him - another him - under the bed staring back at me quivering and whispering "daddy, there's someone in my bed!"

Footprints

One cold winter's night, a young girl called Hannah was at home all alone and just sitting watching the television. Her parents had gone out to a dinner party with their friends. It had been snowing heavily all afternoon, but Hannah felt nice and snug as she sat on the sofa in the living room, tucked up under a warm, fuzzy blanket.

By midnight, Hannah's parents were still not home, and she began to feel a little uneasy. She didn't want to call them, however, just in case they thought that she couldn't take care of herself.

The television was in the corner of the room, right next to some large, glass patio doors leading into the back garden. She was watching the news when a report came on of an escaped murderer in the area, but she thought nothing more of it. Suddenly, out the corner of her eye, she noticed something move by the patio doors.

Through the darkness and the falling snow, she could just make out in the distance the figure of a man, walking slowly towards the window. As he got closer, she was able to make out his face, and it filled her with horror. It was the escaped murderer she had just seen on the news!

The man's face was hideously scarred, his eyes were wild and crazy, and he seemed to be grinning maliciously at her. Feeling frightened and terrified, Hannah pulled the fuzzy blanket over her head, remained absolutely still and completely silent, as she tried to hide. As she peeked through the blanket, she saw that the man was much closer now, as he reached into his coat and pulled out a vicious looking knife!

Hannah frantically pulled the blanket back over her head, hoping that the man would just think she was a pile of blankets thrown onto the sofa, and leave her alone. She managed to move her hand slowly over towards her pocket and took out her mobile phone. Pressing the buttons in a panic, she called the police and held her breath as she waited for an answer.

When the operator asked her "what is your emergency?" Hannah put the phone close to her face and replied, whispering "there's a man outside my window, and he's got a knife - please come quick!" Once Hannah was assured that the police were on their way, she sat there motionless under the blanket.

However, safe in the knowledge that the patio doors were securely locked, and the police were now on their way, Hannah found the confidence to emerge from behind the blanket, march the short distance to the patio doors, and come face to face with her murderous stalker.

She stood there face-to-face with the murderer, with only a pane of glass between them. The murderer raised his knife high above his head, as if to simulate what he would do to her if he could find a way to get inside the property.

Just as she was about to shout at the murderer for him to leave her alone, and that the police were on their way, she noticed something startling. Outside, where the murderer was standing on the snow-covered lawn, the snow was completely undisturbed, and there were no footprints in the snow.

Hannah suddenly realised that the murderer was not standing in the back garden - she was looking at his reflection!

- I thought the eyelash in my eye was causing an unusual amount of pain. Imagine my horror when I watched it burrow back inside!

- Finding myself surrounded by zombies and vampires running towards me, I started shooting them one by one. It totally ruined the Halloween party though!

MY STORY

The following account describes the Author's own personal experience of a creepy and spooky event...

I was alone at home one evening, as my parents were spending a few days away together, and I decided to venture downstairs to get myself a drink from the kitchen. As I reached the bottom of the stairs, I entered the living room, where one single wall light was switched on illuminating the room. I proceeded through to the kitchen, switched the kitchen light on and poured myself a glass of milk.

As I left the kitchen, I switched the kitchen light off and proceeded back through the living room. Just before I left the living room to go back upstairs, I reached out to switch the living room light off - but then stopped short, as I realised that it was only 8pm and I would likely return later for another drink or a snack. So I left this one wall light switched on and continued back upstairs.

Later that evening, about 10pm, I decided to return downstairs for a last drink of milk before going to bed. As I got to the top of the stairs, I noticed that there was no light emanating from the downstairs living room - even though I had left the living room door open and the wall light on so that I could see better coming down the stairs. I could only assume that the bulb had gone.

As I reached the bottom of the stairs, I reached around the door frame expecting the light switch to be in the 'on' position and the bulb to have gone, but instead, the light switch was in the 'off' position. So I proceeded to flick the light switch to the 'on' position, and the wall light came back on.

What was so strange, creepy and bewildering about this event is how I specifically remember leaving the wall light on in the knowledge that I would return downstairs later in the evening. I was certain that I had pulled back from switching the wall light off and returned upstairs.

So how come the wall light was switched off? Who, or what, switched the wall light off?

While the Author can only conclude that he did indeed switch the wall light off, out of sheer habit perhaps, but then returned upstairs thinking he had left it on - to this day, this remains a baffling and spooky event.

ARE YOU BEING HAUNTED?

Many of the stories contained within this book are of a ghostly nature and include all aspects of what may be the work of ghosts, spirits or other entities from the realms of the supernatural. Undoubtedly, having read through each of these 75 scary horror stories, you are now wondering if you have some kind of ghost, spirit or other supernatural being residing in your home? So to put your mind at ease, or to perhaps terrify you even further, we can now take a look at how one might identify the presence of an otherworldly being and determine whether you may indeed have a ghost, a spirit or some other form of supernatural entity, residing in your home...

Do you ever feel that you have an otherworldly presence in your home? Most of us at some point in our lives will experience the weird and strange sensation of seeing shadows and mysterious shapes out the corner of our eye, only for them to disappear when we turn to take a closer look. Such experiences and sensations can be rather unnerving and inexplicable, but whether or not such an event left you feeling spooked and fearful, did you ever stop to wonder exactly what kind of ghostly apparition you just encountered? Perhaps you did not even consider that there could be different kinds of ghosts out there? Well there are many different types of supernatural phenomenon that can occur at any given time, which may be good to know about if you are, or have ever, experienced such ghostly encounters.

Indeed, there are a number of typical signs to know if your house may be haunted by the presence of some kind of ghost, spirit or otherworldly entity. Take your time and explore the following list to see if there are any indicators as to whether or not you have a ghostly presence in your home...

- The floorboards creak when no one else is present in your home.
- Doors appear to open, close and slam shut when you are home alone.
- Furniture is frequently moved from its usual position, but there is no one else around who could have moved it.
- Strange sounds echo through your home at night while you are alone, such as laughter, crying or wailing.
- Parts or the house or property are frequently draughty or experience cold spots, despite the absence of vents or open windows.
- You often see movement and strange shapes in your peripheral vision, which immediately

disappear when you turn around and look sharply.
- Your dog growls or barks viciously - or your cat has a hissing fit - all seemingly random and at nothing in particular.
- Your child becomes emotionally attached to an imaginary friend that they insist is real.
- You actually saw a ghost!

If you have experienced a significant number of these occurrences, without any obvious rational explanation or someone else being around to play tricks on you, then your home may very well be haunted! You can only hope that the ghost, spirit or otherworldly being that inhabits your home is not evil and malevolent in nature, but instead friendly and benevolent.

So how many of these indicators have YOU experienced in your home recently?

DEMONS AND POLTERGEISTS

When it comes to mischief, terror and pure malevolence, there can be no greater force at work more sinister than that of a demon or a poltergeist. One should always be aware of what you can likely expect to occur and experience if you, a loved one or your home is haunted by a demon or a poltergeist...

Demons

One of the most frightening and dangerous kind of spirits that one could find in their home are demons. These otherworldly beings have the ability, and often the desire, to wreak havoc for an individual and their family. Demons are not actually a type of ghost - they are very powerful supernatural beings and non-human spirits. Demons can quite easily disguise themselves as friendly spirits, but they are anything but this! Demons feed off the humans in the household and can sometimes possess the weak-minded - or even attach themselves to inanimate objects. Since demons can disguise themselves and morph into any shape (although they most commonly appear as a black mass standing in doorways), it can be very difficult to identify if you have one residing in your home.

There are two major signs that indicate the presence of a demon...

1. If you or any member of your household is feeling overly lethargic or depressed, this could be a major indicator that a demon is absorbing their energy.
2. If you or any member of your household develops a sudden personality shift (even if it is only for a short amount of time), this could indicate a temporary or long-term demonic possession.

In cases of demonic possession, demons are able to inflict significant mental and physical torture upon its host. When an evil spirit infiltrates a living person, it is able to control their conscious energy - and since they inhabit a physical body, these spirits then have a greater strength than the rest, as they can move objects, hurt people and kill as they please.

Demons are malevolent beings with deeply sinister intentions and are most definitely to be feared!

Poltergeists

Another of the most frightening and dangerous kind of otherworldly beings that one could find in their home are poltergeists. These spirits also have the ability, and often the desire, to wreak havoc for an individual and their family. Being perhaps one of the most popular terms most commonly used when discussing the presence of a ghostly visitor, the term poltergeist literally means 'noisy ghost', because they have the ability to move or knock things over, make noises and violently manipulate the physical environment. While many of us may have heard and used the term 'poltergeist' before, a poltergeist is actually one of the rarest forms of haunting - and for so many, the most terrifying!

If you have ever experienced inexplicable loud knocking sounds, lights turning on and off, find windows and drawers mysteriously open, chairs having moved position, find books knocked from bookshelves, hear doors slamming, find bath and sink taps running, or even fires breaking out without apparent cause, then this kind of spiritual disturbance could indeed be the work of a poltergeist.

Another frightening and disturbing aspect of poltergeist behaviour is that such events usually start out slowly and mildly, leading people to mistake such occurrences for only a strange coincidence or a lapse in memory - but then as time passes, these seemingly trivial events can gradually begin to intensify. While very often poltergeist activity can be rather harmless and end quickly, they have been known to behave with malevolence and can actually become very terrifying and dangerous!

Poltergeist activity can affect an individual psychologically as well as physically. The psychological attacks begin with activities and occurrences that cause fear and anxiety within the victim, thus increasing psychological stress. Of course, this is especially the case when one is the victim of a direct physical attack! Victims can be pushed, tugged or knocked down by an unknown force - or even dragged out of bed, with physical bruises and scars manifesting from such attacks.

Whatever the case may be, poltergeists and poltergeist behaviour have caught the attention of both paranormal investigators and those curious of the phenomenon, with the most common theory being that the existing presence of a living being (often one in emotional turmoil, such as an adolescent teenager) provides the energy that allows the spirit of a poltergeist to interact with the living. As such, removing that person from the home can bring an end to the poltergeist activity - although if another human with a similar kind of energy enters the home, the poltergeist may again use and harness that energy so that it can continue to torment those who reside in the home.

Poltergeists will only ever bring turmoil and despair to your home!

So should you encounter a demon or a poltergeist in your home, please understand that each of these beings are fraught with evil, malevolence and negativity - and they will seek to bring mischief, fear and destruction to your home and tear your family apart!

If you truly believe that you have a demon or a poltergeist residing in your home, it is strongly advised not to try and communicate with it or remove it from your home yourself, for you may only serve to further anger it and cause it to lash out in a fit of rage!

Instead, one should seek the help and guidance of a professional paranormal investigation team that is well experienced in dealing with such matters.

Good luck!

TRADITIONAL GHOSTS

The types of ghosts that are most traditionally talked about are those which appear most commonly in literature and movies. These ghosts tend to haunt either the place in which they died, where they lived, or perhaps even a specific person that they were attached to during their life, such as a spouse or a child. These 'traditional ghosts' are the broadest category of spirits that do not fall under any one specific category of ghost.

Depending on the strength of the ghost, interaction with it can vary drastically. You may be able to see one ghost, but only be able to hear another - and you may not be able to communicate with another ghost at all, but still sense its presence through a sudden and drastic temperature change or the sudden sensation of dread.

Traditional ghosts often have varying motivations for their appearance, such as having 'unfinished business' to complete, which can influence their temperament and be the ultimate reason why they remain among the living. These temperaments can be greatly varying, ranging from the very friendly to the highly dangerous - and the only way to determine their level of danger is through their interactions with the physical world.

The 'holy grail' of all the ghostly photographs captured on camera is the exceptionally rare full body manifestation. These are the images that portray a recognisable human being, in which the subject appears either partially or fully formed and is usually transparent. In some cases, the figure is clear enough to be readily identifiable by the deceased's friends or family, making them even more valuable as evidence of paranormal activity.

Full body manifestations usually appear quite unexpectedly in photographs, most commonly in the background of a picture. In some of the more remarkable cases, they can even appear quite solid, almost as if they are posing for the picture. It is almost like they are either unaware or unwilling to accept their own death, or wish to continue to do the same things they did before death.

There are a number of instances where the image of a family member or a dead soldier appears in a group photo standing behind their still living family or former soldiers, as if they refuse to break the close bonds that exist between families and those who have been through combat together.

Other ghosts, however, seem completely oblivious to the camera and often appear to be simply going about the same routine they maintained while still alive. So while it certainly seems to be the case that some ghosts are quite aware of being photographed, there is no way of knowing whether this is true of all ghosts.

With this in mind, let us now take a look at some of the things you can likely expect to occur if you are witness to an otherworldly visitation, or some form of supernatural and ghostly event...

The Interactive Personality

The most common of all ghostly sightings reported are usually that of a deceased person. This could be someone you know, like a friend or a family member, or perhaps even an historical figure - whether this is someone famous and well-known, or simply someone who resided and perhaps died at that specific location. These ghosts not only appear to be self-aware and intelligent, but they can also be friendly or otherwise and often show themselves in a variety of different ways. They can become visible and walk, or perhaps speak and make noises, or even touch you and emit an odour associated with them (such as tobacco, perfume or aftershave) to let you know of their presence.

These kinds of ghosts often retain their former personality and temperament from when they were alive - and they can still feel emotions, whether they are positive or negative. For this reason, encounters with such ghosts can be a pleasant or a frightening and disturbing experience, depending on the nature of the ghost and the circumstances of its manifestation. In general, however, these kinds of ghosts are harmless and should therefore be treated with due respect and dignity.

Often these ghosts will simply come along and visit you to comfort you, or to convey a message or some information of significant importance. So if you happen to see a lost loved one, then the chances are that they have appeared to you because they feel that you want, or need, to see them one final time - perhaps as a means of saying farewell, with the comforting assurance that 'everything is going to be alright'.

Animal Spirits

Animal ghosts are the spirits of animals that have recently passed. Typically, animal ghosts are that of cats or dogs, but there have also been sightings of other animal species, such as horses and birds.

Animal ghosts are much rarer than the spirits of humans and usually haunt where they lived and not where they died, due to the attachment they had to a particular location. They often linger in their once 'favourite spot' and the areas where they felt the most comfortable, such as near a bed or near their feeding area.

More often than not animal ghosts are only heard and not seen. They occasionally interact with inanimate objects, such as their favourite toy. They may also scratch at doors and walls, or leave an imprint on a bed or wherever they preferred to sleep.

Animal spirits are rarely dangerous and are typically friendly, but even those that are angry or vicious in nature are incapable of harming the living. Unlike some human ghosts, animal ghosts are virtually impossible to connect with, but knowing that they are still around can be somewhat comforting nonetheless.

The Ectoplasm or Ecto-Mist

Have you ever seen a mist or a fog that almost appears like it is swirling around? If so, then you may have been witness to an ectoplasm apparition of a spirit or an otherworldly being, or an ecto-mist that appears in the form of a 'ghostly mist'. This kind of vaporous cloud usually appears several feet from the ground and can stay in one position, or move around very swiftly, while often making the spot or area they are haunting feel remarkably cold.

These ghostly encounters have been captured many times on video recordings and in photographs - and can appear as white, grey or even black in colour. Although such occurrences can appear simply in this way, only to linger and then move away very quickly, sometimes such ectoplasms and ecto-mists can appear before becoming a full-bodied apparition. Many people claim to have witnessed such a phenomenon in graveyards, on former battlefield sites and in historical buildings.

Orbs

Orbs are probably the most photographed and captured kind of anomaly to provide evidence and support for the existence of ghosts. They often manifest themselves as white or blue transparent or translucent shiny balls of light that hover over the ground. Very often one can be completely unaware of them, only to be taken by surprise when someone points one or more of them out in the background of a photo or a video recording that they, or someone else, has taken.

It is commonly believed that orbs are the spiritual energy and 'souls' of human beings (or even animals) that have died and are moving around from one place to another. The circular shape they take on makes it easier for them to move around, and this is often the first state they will appear in before becoming full-bodied apparitions.

Orbs that have been captured on video recordings often make sudden and abrupt movements in different directions, which would suggest that they are neither a natural phenomenon nor mere reflections of light. So if you are lucky enough to capture an orb on video or in a picture, then you will be amazed by how fast and fanciful they can move, and how clear they appear.

Funnel Ghosts or Vortexes

Most often spotted in historical places and old buildings where they once resided, funnel ghosts or 'vortexes' are frequently associated with the sensation of 'cold spots'. Appearing as a wisp of light or a swirling spiral of light, funnel ghosts have also been caught on video and in photographs. They usually take on the shape of a swirling funnel and are most commonly believed to be either the spiritual energy of a loved one returning to visit, or a former resident of the property. In this state, funnel ghosts are believed to be in the final process of manifesting themselves into full-bodied apparitions.

Funnel ghosts and 'vortexes' that have been captured on video recordings often have an eerily unique and unusual pattern of motion that distinguishes them from any natural phenomenon, such as exhaled breath or cigarette smoke. Often they can appear to take on specific and identifiable human forms that one can easily recognise.

So should you encounter any of these kinds of 'traditional ghosts' in your home or elsewhere, it may not always be necessary to remove them from wherever they choose to reside. This is because, for the most part, they are likely to be pleasant and harmless, and are only visiting to make themselves seen, heard and to connect back to the world of the living - and this is not something that one needs to be fearful of.

Perhaps you will choose to embrace their presence? Perhaps you will try talking to them? Perhaps they will choose to answer? What do you think? Do you even dare to try?

GOODNIGHT

If you are witness to any of the ghosts, spirits and otherworldly phenomenon pertaining to the more 'traditional ghosts', then you are much more likely to be in the presence of a friendly and benevolent being - and while this may feel scary and frightening, it may also be completely harmless.

It is the demons and the poltergeists that you need to fear - for these are the beings that bring with them mischief, terror and malevolence!

So while the 75 creepy, spooky and scary horror stories in this book may provide a light-hearted and fun scare for yourself and those you may have chosen to read them to, it is always worth being aware of the noises, activities and strange goings on in your home - or the behaviours of those around you - for you never truly know if, and when, one of these malevolent ghosts, spirits or supernatural beings could come to visit and manifest themselves in YOUR home?

Hopefully, if you are lucky, you will encounter no ghosts at all - and if you do, then they will be one of the friendlier and more benevolent ghosts - but it is the demons and the poltergeists that you really need to be aware of. So always be aware. Be very aware! Because how can you ever be sure whether or not there is some kind of energy or an object in your home that, at this very moment, is attracting a fiendish and frightfully malevolent supernatural being into YOUR home?

How can you ever truly be sure?

                    Goodnight.

ABOUT THE AUTHOR

Steven Parker

Although the Author himself does not personally believe in ghosts, spirits or anything pertaining to the supernatural, one cannot help but feel a little 'spooked' when reading through all of these scary, creepy and rather disturbing horror stories.

With an interest in anything of a ghostly or otherworldly nature, from movies and TV shows to the reading of personal testimonials, the Author has always held a distinct interest in anything that falls within the realms of the supernatural.

The Author can only hope that you, the reader, have enjoyed each of these 75 scary horror stories - and have done so while all alone, and with only the bedside light on, in order to add to one's own anxiety, trepidation and fear!

Hopefully, you still have the nerve to switch the bedside light off and sleep peacefully - free of any disturbing, frightening and terrifying nightmares?

Printed in Dunstable, United Kingdom